ISBN 978-1-331-44911-9
PIBN 10191648

This book is a reproduction of an important historical work. Forgotten Books uses
state-of-the-art technology to digitally reconstruct the work, preserving the original format
whilst repairing imperfections present in the aged copy. In rare cases, an imperfection in
the original, such as a blemish or missing page, may be replicated in our edition. We do,
however, repair the vast majority of imperfections successfully; any imperfections that
remain are intentionally left to preserve the state of such historical works.

1 MONTH OF
FREE
READING

at

www.ForgottenBooks.com

By purchasing this book you are eligible for one month membership to ForgottenBooks.com, giving you unlimited access to our entire collection of over 700,000 titles via our web site and mobile apps.

To claim your free month visit:

www.forgottenbooks.com/free191648

English
Français
Deutsche
Italiano
Español
Português

www.forgottenbooks.com

Mythology Photography **Fiction**
Fishing Christianity **Art** Cooking
Essays Buddhism Freemasonry
Medicine **Biology** Music **Ancient**
Egypt Evolution Carpentry Physics
Dance Geology **Mathematics** Fitness
Shakespeare **Folklore** Yoga Marketing
Confidence Immortality Biographies
Poetry **Psychology** Witchcraft
Electronics Chemistry History **Law**
Accounting **Philosophy** Anthropology
Alchemy Drama Quantum Mechanics
Atheism Sexual Health **Ancient History**
Entrepreneurship Languages Sport
Paleontology Needlework Islam
Metaphysics Investment Archaeology
Parenting Statistics Criminology
Motivational

BOYISH REMINISCENCES OF HIS MAJESTY THE KING'S VISIT TO CANADA IN 1860

THOMAS BUNBURY GOUGH, MIDSHIPMAN, H.M.S. "HERO"

Frontispiece

BOYISH REMINISCENCES OF HIS MAJESTY THE KING'S VISIT TO CANADA IN 1860

BY LIEUT. THOMAS BUNBURY GOUGH, R.N.

THEN A MIDSHIPMAN ON H.M.S. "HERO"

WITH ILLUSTRATIONS

LONDON

JOHN MURRAY, ALBEMARLE STREET, W.

1910

PREFACE

SHORTLY after the accession of His Majesty King Edward, these reminiscences of my dear husband, Lieutenant Gough, R.N., appeared in the *Sun*, a Melbourne weekly newspaper. In accordance with a widely expressed wish, their publication in book form was determined upon, but the untimely death of the writer intervened and prevented it being attempted.

Lieutenant Gough had intended to come to London to arrange for the publication, as he wanted to get permission from the proprietors of the *Illustrated London News* to reproduce the pictures by their special artist, Mr. W. H. Andrews, R.W.S., who was chosen to illustrate the royal visit to Canada.

That permission was most graciously accorded

by the present proprietor when circumstances permitted me to visit London to carry out what death had unhappily prevented my husband from accomplishing.

EVELYN GOUGH.

CONTENTS

vii

CHAPTER VI

CHAPTER VII

CHAPTER VIII

CHAPTER IX

CHAPTER X

CHAPTER XI

LIST OF ILLUSTRATIONS

xi

BOYISH REMINISCENCES OF HIS MAJESTY THE KING'S VISIT TO CANADA IN 1860

CHAPTER I

Her Majesty Queen Victoria consents to allow His Royal Highness Albert Edward, Prince of Wales, to visit Canada—H.M.S. *Hero* chosen to carry the illustrious passenger.

In 1860, in compliance with a long-standing promise by the Queen, the Prince of Wales visited Canada; the circumstances which led to the promise being given are at the present time almost forgotten, but, in justice to Canada, they ought to be remembered. Our Colonies excited great enthusiasm by the part they took during the South African War, but Canada bears the proud distinction that during the Crimean War, fifty-five years ago, she was ready to show, and did show, her loyalty to the Empire by raising and equipping at her own expense a regiment of infantry, which was incorporated into the British Army as the 100th Regiment, or Royal Canadians, being now the 1st Battalion of the Leicester Regiment.

In response to the Queen's desire to know how such loyalty could be rewarded, the Canadians pleaded for a personal visit from Her Majesty, but State reasons at that time precluded the lengthened absence of the Sovereign that such a visit would entail. The Queen, however, gave a promise that as soon as the Prince of Wales was old enough, and his education would permit of it, he should pay a visit to the loyal colonists.

In 1860 a great engineering work was just approaching completion, the Victoria Bridge over the St. Lawrence at Montreal, built by the Canadian Grand Trunk Railway, and the request of the Canadian Government to the Queen to allow the promised visit of the Prince of Wales to take place in time to declare the bridge open made a fitting opportunity for a royal visit to Canada. The consent of Her Majesty was given, and the Canadians determined to receive the Prince in right royal style.

Various ways were suggested to convey the Prince across the Atlantic. The royal yacht, a Cunard liner, even the Great Eastern, were all proposed and abandoned. At last the Admiralty determined to send the Prince over in a man-of-war, and H.M.S. *Hero*, on board which ship the writer had the honour to be serving as midshipman, was chosen for the purpose.

The *Hero* was a screw line-of-battle ship of 91 guns, 600 h.p., and had a complement of 800 officers and men. She was considered a crack ship of her class, and was serving her first commission in the Channel Fleet. She was commanded by Captain G. H. Seymour, C.B., whose family influence at Court had no little voice in the *Hero* being picked out for the honour of conveying the Prince on his visit. Captain Seymour's sister was about to be married to Her Majesty's nephew, Prince Victor of Hohenlohe.

In March, 1860, the Channel Fleet had been ordered to Lisbon. The *Hero*, however, did not accompany the fleet, having been detained at Spithead for some purpose. She sailed about ten days afterwards, and, making a rapid passage under sail all the way, joined the fleet in the Tagus. We were just in three days, and were enjoying the oranges and donkey-riding so dear to the heart of a midshipman, when the English mail steamer came in. A signal from the flagship, the *Royal Albert*, for our Captain was made, and after half an hour's visit he came back, sent for the Commander, and ordered him to prepare for sea with all despatch.

Great was the wonder in the gun-room mess when we heard we were off again. One midshipman came down with a long face, and said the Captain's coxswain had told him that we were ordered to Plymouth, there to complete with stores and reinforce the Chinese Squadron. He was promptly kicked out of the gun-room by our senior midshipman, who had just completed a three years' commission on the China station, and had lost an eye there, so had no liking even for the hint. However, all our surmises were put to an end by a thunderous stampede of feet outside the gun-room bulkhead. A shrill pipe and a bellow of " Clear lower deck!" a quartermaster putting his head inside the door and informing us, " Unmoor ship, gen'l'men; commander wants to see all young gen'l'men at their stations," cleared the gun-room too.

An hour or two afterwards we were steaming down the Tagus, passing old Belem Castle, and that night we were under all plain sail for Plymouth. On arrival there, we found that the cause of our recall home was for the purpose of being fitted out to convey H.R.H. the Prince of Wales to Canada. A few days afterwards we steamed up into Hamoaze, and our men and officers hulked on board the *Vigo*, an old Spanish line-of-battle ship, the *Hero* being docked at Keyham, and put in the hands of the dockyard people to make the necessary alterations for the comfort of our illustrious passenger.

The work of fitting out the ship for the reception of H.R.H. the Prince of Wales proceeded rapidly. A large suite was going with the Prince, and extensive accommodation had to be provided. The main-deck guns as far forward as the mainmast were dismounted, the carriages were struck into the hold, the guns themselves were securely lashed fore and aft in the water-ways, and cabins built. The ward-room was reserved for the high officials who were going out with the Prince, the ward-room officers were relegated to the port side of the gun-room, while the midshipmen had the starboard side, a fore and aft bulkhead separating the two messes. The Captain's quarters under the poop were reserved for the Prince. The fittings were plain but comfortable, the sleeping and after cabins being lined with a pretty pattern of chintz picked out by the Queen. The two 32-pounder guns were painted white and gold. The fact that the ship was a man-of-war was strictly kept in view; the first sight the Prince saw in the morning when he awoke was the breech of one of the guns at the foot of his cot, to remind him that he was on board one of his mother's ships, and as secure as if he were in the heart of the kingdom.

A short description of the personnel of the officers and men of the *Hero* may not here seem out of place. I have already mentioned our Captain, but the Commander is the executive officer of a large man-of-war, and much depends on him as to the discipline and well-being of the ship. Our Commander, G. H. Stirling, was well known in Australia, his father being Admiral Stirling, once Governor of West Australia, and he himself afterwards Commodore of the Australian station. He married a Sydney lady, Miss Deas Thomson. He was a splendid officer and seaman. The very look of him was enough to inspire confidence: short, dark, and squarely built, he looked like a bantam-cock. There were two midshipmen in our mess who had served a previous commission with him in a sloop-of-war on the south-east coast of America, and they used to say that any midshipman he took a fancy to he would work off his feet just to show his appreciation of him. I certainly must have been in his good books; I was midshipman of the quarter-deck quarters, midshipman of the maintop, midshipman of the first cutter, besides several other lighter billets thrown in just to take up my spare time. As for the naval instructor, I never saw him even once a week. He one day approached the Commander with a request that I might be excused some ship duty to attend instruction in the fore-cabin, but whatever answer he got I could not tell, except that he beat a hasty retreat down the poop ladder. All our other officers were men who had seen service in the Black Sea, Baltic, Indian Mutiny, and China. Amongst our Lieutenants was Viscount Kilcoursie, who afterwards became Earl of Cavan, and died in 1900. He was Lieutenant of my watch, and a first-class seaman and officer. When it became known that we were being fitted out to convey the Prince of Wales to Canada, many applications were made by men to join, and we started to weed out all the bad eggs. Ships were paying off, and we had our pick, so that as we approached completion we had got together a magnificent ship's company, all veteran seamen, and most of them medalled men. We had one Victoria Cross man amongst them; curious to

or Lucknow Siege *a Nova Scotian convo*

say, he was a negro, by name William Hall. V.C.'s were not so plentiful then as they are now.

Particular attention was given to our band, and our Second-Lieutenant, R. M. Blomfield, a son of the Bishop of London, who was a bit of a musician, was given *carte blanche* to bring it up equal to the occasion. Extra bandsmen were entered, and we had a band of about fifty strong, certainly by far the best naval band that I have ever heard. Our bandmaster, Pritchard, was afterwards honoured on the return of the Prince by being offered the post of first clarionet in the Queen's private band. However, he stuck to the ship, and I afterwards met him in Auckland, New Zealand, as bandmaster of the *Galatea*, H.R.H. the Duke of Edinburgh's ship.

As regards our marines, of whom we had 150, they were nearly all bronzed veterans; we had a few "Queen's hard bargains" among them, which we got rid of to headquarters, not before, however, one of them fell in badly. The incident was ludicrous in itself, but disastrous to the marine. As he happened to be my servant, and as I was an actor in the scene, I will relate what happened to the midshipman and the marine, with the boatswain's mate thrown in at the finale.

CHAPTER II

My marine servant

EVERY midshipmen has a marine servant told off to look after his belongings. As a rule the marine is a steady man, and is a sort of sea-father to his youthful master. My marine, how-ever, was anything but a steady fellow, and nearly always had his leave stopped for some offence against discipline. His name was Joseph Hull. He was a capital servant, and I was always turned out in tiptop style. My sea-chest in the steerage was always laid out in apple-pie order. Mr. Hull had a key to the steerage, the midshipman's sleeping and dress-ing-room; also a key to my chest, that he might take out my clothes to brush. After attending to their masters, the marine servants went about their duties.

I have already stated that the *Hero's* ship's company were hulked on board the old *Vigo*, the *Hero* being in dock at Keyham. We sent large working-parties to the dockyard every forenoon and afternoon. No men were allowed out of the dockyard unless passed out by a petty or non-commissioned officer. As I have said, Joseph Hull's leave was stopped, and many a longing glance he cast at the dockyard gates, but nobody passed *him* out. One forenoon, when the working-parties had returned at seven bells (half-past eleven) to dinner, the sergeant of marines in charge of the dockyard party reported that Joseph Hull was absent. On return to the dockyard no trace of him could be found, and it became evident that Mr. Hull had, by some ingenious method, evaded the dockyard police, and got out. The method will appear later on. The usual description of the absent man was sent to the Plymouth police, and things went on as usual. Next day I was down in the gun-room. We had just finished dinner, when the quartermaster of the watch came down and said the Commander wanted

Mr. Gough on the poop. Wondering what scrape I had got myself into, and cudgelling my brains for any dereliction of duty, I made my way up on the poop, and found the officer of the watch and the Commander inspecting the signal-slate, which the signalman on duty was holding out for their inspection. As I came up the poop-ladder, the Commander gave a sharp glance at me, whilst the officer of the watch turned away with a broad grin. " Come here, Mr. Gough," said the Commander. " Do you know anything about this signal?" As he spoke he took the signal-slate from the signal-man, and held it out to me. I could see that he was in a towering rage, and, taking the slate, I read: " Send escort to Mount Wise guard-room for Mr. Gough, midshipman of *Hero*, who is a prisoner there " I looked at the slate and then at the commander, and then at the slate again. " Now, look here, Mr. Gough; if this is any of your midshipman's pranks, I will put you under arrest and report you to the Captain," said the Commander. But I disclaimed all knowledge of the signal. " Very extra-ordinary," said the Commander. "Here; make a signal that Mr. Gough is on board his ship." In a few minutes back came the answer: "Send Mr. Gough with escort." "Well," said the Commander, "you had better get ready to go on shore with the escort at two bells" (one o'clock). I went below to the gun-room, where my messmates were eager to know the cause of my being sent for by the Commander, and, on hearing my story, they greeted it with roars of laughter. However, orders had to be obeyed; so, going to the gun-room door, I told the sentry on duty there to pass the word along for my new marine. He soon appeared, to know the cause of his being sent for. Telling him I had to go on shore on duty at two bells, and that I wanted my best uniform laid out and my chest got ready for dressing, he disappeared. Presently he came back again. "Beg pardon, sir, I can't find no other uniform in your chest."

"What?" said I.

"Can't find no other uniform in your chest, sir," repeated the marine amid the roars of laughter of my messmates. I stood staring at my servant, whilst he stood upright, stiff as a poker, waiting for instructions.   Time was getting on; in a few minutes the hands would be turned up, and the Commander roaring out, " Where was Mr. Gough ?"

Rapidly making my way to the steerage, followed by my marine, I got to my chest, and, assisted by him, I had all my belongings out, but no trace of the missing uniform; no doubt a theft had been committed.   Sending for the master-at-arms, who is chief of the ship's police, I told my tale.

" Ha," said Rowe, the master-at-arms, " Hull, the missing marine, was your servant, wasn't he, sir ?"

" Yes," said I.

" Well, he has stolen your clothes, no doubt," said the master-at-arms.

Mentally and vocally cursing Mr. Hull, I proceeded to make a rapid toilet, and had a brush down, as the uniform I wore had a fine coating of dockyard dust.   Opening the receptacle where I kept my caps, I found my best uniform cap was gone, too.   Invoking another blessing on the suspected thief, I made my way up the hatchway just as it struck two bells, which was followed by the shrill pipe of eight boatswains' mates and a roar of "All hands!" On reaching the quarter-deck, I reported myself to the officer of the watch, who was standing by the Commander. The latter took a rapid survey of me.

"Have you got no better uniform than that, youngster?" said he.

"If you please, sir, my best uniform has been stolen out of my chest."

"Stolen!" said the Commander, "by whom?"

"The master-at-arms thinks it was Hull, the missing marine, who was my servant, sir," I said.

"I shouldn't wonder," he said; "he's blackguard enough for anything. I know him of old. Well," he went on, "you look as if you were paying off in a ten-gun brig from the West Coast of Africa, instead of a midshipman of a smart line-of-battle ship. But here, get out of this, and get on shore; the boat is manned, and waiting alongside."

Touching my shabby old cap, I went to the gangway, where the escort of two marines and a corporal, fully accoutred, were waiting. They went down the side, followed by me, and we took our seats in the launch, which was in charge of one of our senior midshipmen. There was a suppressed titter amongst the launch's crew, who sat with their oars tossed up. The story had evidently got wind. It is wonderful how fast news travels in a man-of-war.

After giving the orders, " Shove off, for'ard !" " Down !" " Give way together !" my brother-mid turned to me. He was an Honourable, and bore an historic name, a ripping good fellow, and had seen a great deal of service, having been in the trenches before Sebastopol in the Naval Brigade.

"Well, old man," he said, " this is quite an adventure of yours."

"Yes," I replied shortly, thinking of my stolen uniform.

" I would not mind someone stealing my uniform," continued he.

" Why ?" I asked.

" Why !" he exclaimed. " Why, you blessed ass!" (it wasn't blessed, but something stronger), " you will want a lot of new things for the Prince, and you can write a strong letter to your governor, telling him all about it, and saying you must have a new outfit."

I had never looked at my loss in that light, but I thought I would act on my messmate's hint.

In a few minutes more the launch sheered alongside the dockyard steps, and the escort and myself landed. Telling the corporal that I would follow them up to Mount Wise, I made my way to Batten and Adams, the Devonport naval outfitters, where I had an account, and in a few minutes I had on a brand-new uniform, and made my way to solve the riddle.

On arriving at the guard-room, I found the escort there before me, with the sergeant of the guard in conversation with our corporal.

" Now, sergeant, where is this prisoner of yours that calls himself Mr. Gough of the *Hero* ?" said I—" because I am Mr. Gough."

" Well, sir, we don't know rightly who he

is," the sergeant replied, " because, you see, sir, he calls himself an hofficer, and gave your name ; besides, he's in uniform."

" Where is he now ?" I asked.

" In the guard-house, sir ; asleep he is, sir," answered the sergeant. " He was very drunk, sir, when they brought him here."

" Who brought him ?" I asked

" Why, the police, sir. He stole a pair of boots hout of a shop, and they brought him along 'ere," said the sergeant.

" Let us see the fellow; come along, corporal." The sergeant led the way, closely followed by myself, and the corporal unlocked the large guard-room cell. There lay a figure stretched out on the wooden guard-bed or bench. It was Hull, clad in my missing uniform, filthy dirty, torn in several places, with a crusting of mud where the wearer had indulged in a drunken wallow. It was with mingled feelings of disgust and anger that I surveyed the scamp.

Hearing voices, he opened his eyes, and seeing me with the corporal, he scrambled to his feet, giving several drunken lurches in the process; it

was evident he was still half under the influence
of his recent potations. When he did at last
stand upright, he certainly presented a unique
appearance. I was a boy of about five feet
four inches, he was a man of at least six feet.
My trousers were half up to his knees, the
jacket-sleeves too short by six inches, my best
cap stuck on the back of his head, and the
waistcoat was tied across with a bootlace.

"Hullo, Mr. Gough!" said he; "how are
yer?" (hiccough). "Begs yer pardon for a-
making use of yer togs" (hiccough), "but, Lord,
I have had a rare good spree! Spec's I'll get
four bag [dozen] for it" (hiccough).

"Now, Hull," said the corporal, "pull yourself together; you have got to come along of us;"
and the corporal produced a pair of handcuffs to
put on his prisoner. I objected to the man
going through the streets handcuffed in a midshipman's uniform. "Well, sir," asked the
corporal, "what ham I to do?"

"Do?" I replied. "I don't know what you
are to do. Send one of your men down to the
Marine Barracks, and see if you can't get hold

of an old blue jumper and trousers, with a forage cap."

We were now outside the guard-house, and the corporal walked over to where his two men were waiting. After a consultation with them, back he came to me.

"Beg parding, sur, we be Chatham division men, and don't know nobody down at the barracks."

I knew this must be the case, so, telling the corporal to wait, I walked outside into the street. I was determined that Hull should not go through the streets in what was once my uniform, but what was I to do? Midshipmen are generally resourceful boys, and all sorts of expedients came into my mind—wrap him up in a blanket; get three sacks, and rig him out in them. I thought them all out, but where were the sacks to come from? At last I thought I would go down to the barracks myself. I had met some of the junior marine officers, and had dined at the mess. When I got there, I asked if Mr. S. was in barracks; luckily, he happened to be orderly officer of the day. I sent up my name, and he came along at once, inviting me up to the anteroom, where, over a drink and a cigar, I told my tale, interrupted by shouts of laughter. My friend said he would do what he could, and, leaving me, came back in a minute or two with the Adjutant. I was made to repeat my story for his edification. However, the Adjutant sent for the storekeeper, and the necessary articles of attire were procured from some deserter's effects, and sent down to the guard-room. By this time Mr. Hull was pretty sober, and was made to take off my things and don the deserter's, and, being handcuffed, was marched down to the dockyard, I following on the other side of the street. A boat was sent on shore for us. On arrival on board Hull was put in irons. I went down to the gun-room, where I was chaffed unmercifully.

Next morning Hull was brought up before the Commander. The Captain was on Admiralty leave, and the Commander was supreme. The charge of breaking out of the dockyard and stealing an officer's clothes was preferred against him. It appears he opened my chest, made my uniform into a neat bundle, went with the working party and concealed himself in the dockyard, put my clothes on, and walked boldly out of the gates as an officer in spite of the appearance he presented.

After spending what money he possessed in beer, to replenish his exchequer he helped himself to a pair of boots from a boot-shop in Union Street. The shopman saw him, and gave chase. Hull, carrying a heavy press of grog and beer, made off, but was soon collared by a policeman, and the boots were given back to their rightful owner. As the policeman got hold of him he turned round and said, "What do yer mean by laying 'ands on a hofficer?"

He made no defence to the charge, and had nothing to say. The Commander looked at him for a minute or so. "Four dozen lashes." Then to the clerk, "Make out a warrant."

Hull was marched off. Next morning the gratings were rigged. The hands turned up "to witness punishment," and Hull got as good a four dozen as ever was given in the Royal Navy, which he took as unconcernedly as if his back was of leather. I have never seen a marine give any sign of distress under corporal punishment. It is a matter of honour with them. As Hull was certainly not an acquisition to our almost picked ship's company, an opportunity was made of getting rid of him to headquarters, and I never saw him again; but Gough and his servant were a standing joke in the gun-room mess during the remainder of the commission.

I am afraid that the above story can hardly be called "a reminiscence of His Majesty." It is, however, a true one of his Navy, as I knew it.

CHAPTER III

THE fittings of the *Hero* were now almost complete, and on June 1, 1860, the officers and men were turned over from the old *Vigo* to their own ship. The work of painting, setting up rigging, and all the hundred and one things that are always to be done on board a man-of-war, were effected by our men. The dockyard people always leave a ship in a dirty state, and Plymouth Dockyard "mateys," as they are termed, are proverbial for dirt. Heaps of chips, shavings, and other odds and ends were to be discovered in all sorts of out-of-the-way places. But nothing escaped our Argus-eyed Commander; he was ubiquitous. You might be standing down on the orlop deck, when there was a quick, smart tread, and along he came with the gunner or carpenter. If you fell under his eye, it was, "Young gentleman, what are you doing here?" and whoever the gentleman was, he soon got packed off about some duty. As for the boat midshipmen, they were backwards and forwards all day long. I don't know how many tons of sand and holystones I took off, but I should imagine that they must have taken about an inch off the decks if they were all used. A good many of them found their way overboard out of the lower deck ports. If there is one thing more than another that a bluejacket hates, it is a holystone. To go down on his knees and grind slowly away at the deck with a lump of stone weighing about five pounds is not conducive to a man's temper, especially if, when he stops for a moment to have a short yarn with the next man to him, or turn his quid, there is a shout from the midshipman · "Now then, keep those holystones going! Where's the boy with sand? Here, boy; more sand there!"

The gun-room officers found their mess-place cut in half, and it was a tight squeeze to pack about thirty-four midshipmen, mates, etc., in such a small space, which was also curtailed by two 8-inch guns and carriages. We did not mind the want of room so much as the close proximity to the ward-room officers, who had the port side of the gun-room. There was always some noisy game going on at night among the midshipmen, vingt-et-un and blind hookey being the favourites. Yells and shouts of " I'll stand !" " Another !" etc., used to disturb the staid members of the ward-room mess. There was only a thin bulkhead between the two messes. At last a mild request from the ward-room would come through the sentry at the gun-room door, perhaps from the chaplain : " Would the gun-room officers kindly make a little less noise ?" An interjection from the senior mate or midshipman—" Less noise there, you fellows in the corner !" After a few minutes of comparative quiet, another outbreak, followed by not a request this time, but an order from one of the Lieutenants—" The gun-room officers to make less noise !"

" Too bad !" growls the senior, as he takes a

stride towards the offending card-party, who disperse in all directions. One jumps over a gun, another dives under a table, while a third receives a cuff on the head with the intimation that if there is any more of it the whole party will be kicked off to their hammocks.

Another quiet quarter of an hour, during which play is conducted in undertones; then another yell and shout.

Again the sentry puts his head in. "Commander's orders, gentlemen: if there is any more noise, he will have the gun-room lights put out and the mess cleared."

This puts a stopper on the card-playing youths, and the cards are put away, and comparative quiet reigns—that is, if a midshipman of those days could be quiet.

However, we have to be getting ready for sea, for it is time His Majesty was well under way for Canada. The ship was to be inspected by the Commander-in-Chief, Vice-Admiral Sir A. Fanshawe, on July 1, and things were rapidly approaching completion.

At last came a beautiful Sunday, when the

last nail had been driven and the last paint-brush put away, and H.M.S. *Hero* floated on the calm waters of Hamoaze, a perfect picture of a ship. I shall never forget that Sunday. It was my forenoon watch. The trees on the beautiful slopes of Mount Edgcumbe were clad in their full summer foliage. A gentle breeze rippled the water. It was a true West-Country summer's day. We were waiting to muster by divisions. The dear old ship was a credit to everyone belonging to her. She was always a handsome ship, perhaps the handsomest line-of-battle ship in the service—at least, I always thought so. Old Poole, our boatswain, had been round the ship twice. The yards were as square as if a spirit-level had been used. Every rope in the vast network of rigging was as taut as a harp-string. Inboard everything looked equally well. The snow-white decks, the polished guns, the long line of white hammocks, the boats, with the Prince's feathers on their bows, were all perfect in their way, and the *Hero* looked fit for the mission she had been picked out for.

Two days afterwards we were inspected by
the Admiral, who complimented Captain Seymour on the fine appearance of the ship and
ship's company. Another and final inspection
by the First Sea Lord of the Admiralty, and we
had received our hall-mark   Next day we
steamed into Plymouth Sound and anchored.
We had some final preparations to make. The
day after we went into the Sound our consort,
the *Ariadne*, joined us. She was a splendid
26-gun frigate, sister-ship to the *Galatea*, afterwards commanded by the Duke of Edinburgh.
The *Ariadne* was under the command of Captain
E. W. Vansittart, an officer, a seaman, and a
gentleman, every inch of him. I served a commission with him afterwards, and ought to
know. The other vessel of the Royal Squadron
was the *Flying Fish*, a first-class despatch gun-
vessel of six guns, commanded by Commander
C. W. Hope. But she had already sailed for
America, as her speed was slow, and she
wanted more time than the heavier ships.
On July 3 our Captain hoisted his broad blue
pendant as Commodore of the second class,

which was duly saluted by the *Ariadne* with nine guns.

A word here may explain the various colours then in use in the navy. Now the navy only flies one colour—viz., the white ensign; at the time I write of there were Admirals, Vice-Admirals, and Rear-Admirals, of the red, the white, and the blue. Red was the royal colour, the red ensign being flown by the royal yachts. We had a special set of colours for the Prince's trip issued to us. When he was on board, we used to fly his standard, with its quaint heraldic device in the centre, and the red ensign; when not on board, our Commodore's blue colours. We had gorgeous silk standards and colours for State occasions, such as landing, etc.

The Prince was to embark on July 9, and we were busy taking in all sorts of stores; our after-magazine, instead of combustibles, carried comestibles. There were no refrigerating chambers in those days. The Prince's and suite's tables were the special care of a mess-man, Mr. Parkes. Nearly all the provisions were tinned—the best that the great London and French houses could supply. The Emperor of the French sent a contribution in the shape of some wonderful preserved Swiss milk. It was ripping good stuff, as I found out, for the kind-hearted Prince's messman often sent a bottle of it into the gun-room.

On the 7th another Swiss article made its way on board, but this time it was live-stock, in the shape of a royal Swiss courier in a wonderful get-up of green and gold; he took a final look through the Prince's cabins, and went on shore again.

At last the day arrived which we had so long looked for. It was a beautiful morning, and it was my morning watch. I was up on the poop with my shoes and stockings off, looking after the mizzen-top men as they washed down the poop. I saw the signalman of the watch looking through his glass to seaward. In a minute or two I saw him bend on the " demand," and next minute it was flying from our main truck.

I may say that the " demand " is a signal between men-of-war to ask the names of ships. Asking him what he saw, he gave me his glass, and pointed out where I was to look, and just on the horizon I could see the top-gallant sails of a great fleet. It was the Channel Fleet, waiting for the royal yacht.

By five o'clock everything was ready. The men dressed in best blue trousers, white frocks, and blue jackets, with black hats; all officers in full uniform, life-lines on for manning yards, salute loaded; crimson silk man-ropes on the accommodation-ladder, which was also covered with crimson cloth. We waited, but no royal yacht.

I must confess I was a bit nervous. I was only a boy of fifteen, and had been brought up to regard royalty as above ordinary humanity. I had seen the Queen at a distance, passing in her yacht, at Portsmouth, but now I was to be brought into immediate contact with the future King of England; then I thought of home, and my dear old dad talking about "My boy, sir, with H.R.H. the Prince of Wales, sir," blowing out his cheeks and talking as if he had the credit of the whole royal visit, bless him!

All my nervousness and thoughts of home

were knocked on the head by the thunder of guns at sea. There was a rush of officers to the poop; it was the Channel Fleet saluting the royal yacht. In about an hour she was in sight, and rapidly approached. It was six o'clock when she passed the eastern end of the break-water; as she did so we manned yards and saluted. She anchored close to us, and a signal was made that the Prince would embark on board us at seven o'clock, so the men were called down from aloft and sent below. A quarter to seven they were called up again, the marines under arms, with their Captain, or, rather, Brevet-Major, old David Blyth, who always used to put me in mind of Colonel Newcome; the band and drums on the poop, all officers on the quarter-deck, and everything ready. Our Commander had one trouble: he was afraid the band would only play one bar of the National Anthem instead of two for a royal salute, and he reminded our bandmaster several times when waiting by holding up two fingers.

At last we saw the *Victoria and Albert's* barge manned, and our royal passenger left the yacht with the Prince Consort, and approached the *Hero*. As they did, " Man yards!" was ordered, the men facing aft, as the royal yacht was astern of the *Hero*. As they came close the boatswain piped the side, and eight junior midshipmen in full dress acted as side-boys. As the men on the yard are not supposed to turn their backs on royalty, the order was given, " Mizzen-mast there, face for'ard!" and the Jacks performed the acrobatic feat of right-about-turn in mid-air, this bringing them facing the quarter-deck. Another pause. We hear the boat alongside, the Commodore advances to the gangway, the Commander holds up a warning two fingers again to the band as he turns. " A royal salute. Present arms!" orders old David Blyth. One hundred and fifty bayonets leap into the air, the Commodore, cocked hat in hand, bows almost to the deck, the band and drums crash out, and H.R.H. the Prince Consort steps on to the quarter-deck, followed by a slight boyish figure with a pleasant face, who, with a hearty laugh, greets the Commodore. This was our royal passenger, who to-day is His Majesty King

Edward VII., God bless him! The royal pair were followed by the Duke of Newcastle, Secretary of State for the Colonies; the Earl of St. Germans, Lord Steward; Major-General Bruce, the Prince's Governor; Dr. Acland; Major Teesdale, R.A., V.C., and Captain Grey, of the Grenadier Guards, equerries to the Prince. They were all to accompany him. The whole party, preceded by the Commodore, made their way to the Prince's quarters, under the poop. After an inspection, the Prince Consort and Prince expressed their entire approval of them. An impromptu levee was then held in the forecabin, each officer of the ship being presented by name to Their Royal Highnesses.

The Prince Consort and Prince of Wales took their stand in the forecabin, surrounded by the suite. The Commodore called out each officer's name, who came forward by the starboard door, bowed, and retired backwards through the port door. It was rather ludicrous to watch how some of our officers tried to preserve their balance in stepping backward. We all acquitted ourselves very well. One officer, however, overran his distance, and, forgetting to allow for the door-ledge at the retiring door, hit it with his heels, and disappeared backward through the door with a tremendous crash, presenting to the Prince a pair of heels and the bottoms of a pair of gold-laced trousers. After the levee was over, Their Royal Highnesses retired to the after-cabin, where a quiet farewell hour was spent. On leaving the cabin, I joined my messmates on the quarter-deck, where we discussed the levee, each mid describing how he executed his particular sternboard out of the cabin, the officer who came to grief receiving a deal of good-natured chaff.

Whilst we were thus engaged, our attention was attracted to the gangway. A blaze of colour lit up the scene. We had been a little disappointed at not seeing any of our distinguished visitors in uniform; all were in plain morning-dress, even to the equerries. But here we had our wishes gratified to the utmost. A group of royal and ducal servants were standing at the gangway, no less than seventeen of them. They were clad in gorgeous raiment, from the crimson

6

and gold of the palace to the modest brown of the doctor's valet. They were wondering which way to turn, and were regarding everybody with an air of calm superiority which excited the merriment of the midshipmen. One of them, an elderly man of vast proportions, who appeared to be the leader, advanced towards us. I don't know what he took us for at that stage—probably cabin-boys—but we beat a discreet retreat.

It was getting dusk at the time, and we got below to the gun-room. Then over the Queen's allowance of half a gill of rum we again discussed the events of the day, and also the advisability of bringing the palace retainers to a sense of our importance. The service, we maintained, would go to the dogs (it wasn't dogs, but something else commencing with a d——) if it were not for the midshipmen. We were all going to be Lord Nelsons. The Prince's brother was a midshipman, and if these fellows didn't know, they would have to be taught, etc. In fact, the discussion, what between rum and indignation, became so animated that our senior mate chipped in: "Here, what are you youngsters gabbling about? What are you doing down here? You're all on duty. Clear out on deck; you'll be wanted directly!" He didn't say what he was doing down in the gun-room himself, but we obeyed orders.

Just as we reached the door three smart taps of a drum on the main-deck gave notice that the marine guard were required on deck, and that the Prince Consort was about to leave the ship. All the officers were on deck again; the guard under arms with the band; a long line of battle-lanterns lit up the quarter-deck. The Prince Consort said farewell to the Prince of Wales at the gangway, and was rowed over to the *Victoria and Albert*, on board of which he was going to pass the night.

A few minutes afterwards two bells (nine o'clock) pealed out, the Commodore's gun was fired, the Last Post began to wail out from the bugles, the rounds gone, and quiet settled down on the *Hero* with her illustrious freight on board.

CHAPTER IV

The departure—His Royal Highness's suite—
"Man overboard!"

THE 10th of July, 1860, the day on which
H.R.H. the Prince of Wales was to take his
departure from the shores of England, dawned
calm and clear. On board H.M.S. *Hero* the
hands had been turned up at four o'clock. I
was roused by a tug at the clews of my
hammock and the announcement of my hammock-man "It's gone two bells, sir. The
guard and steerage 'ammocks been piped up,
sir."

I noticed that most of my messmates had
turned out, and that their hammocks were being
lashed up—very different this morning from the
usual routine enacted in the steerage on other
mornings, when the above announcement had
to be repeated many times by the unfortunate

40

hammock-man, sitting patiently on his master's sea-chest, as Mr. Sleepyhead took another round turn in the blankets.

The various sounds of preparation for sea resounded throughout the ship. A low, vibrating hum told of steam being got up; the rattle of chain as the messenger was passed, combined with the clatter of capstan-bars, struck a varied medley of sounds on the ear, while the nose was saluted with the fragrant smell of the breakfast cocoa in the ship's coppers. The latter had more attractions for a midshipman, who is always hungry.

I made my way to the gun-room, where a party of messmates were each discussing a big basin of ship's cocoa with a flint-like biscuit. Various subjects were the theme of conversation the events of yesterday; when we were going to get under way; whose forenoon watch it was —when one mid. struck in with, "Anyone seen old 'Twenty Stun' this morning?"

"Who's 'Twenty Stun'?" said another.

"Oh, you ass!" was the reply. "Why, the big old palace fellow we saw last night."

"Oh, *him*. No, nobody has seen him, you may be sure. Too early for him," was the other's answer.

A flap or two of the screw under our feet now told us that steam was up. At the same time a long-drawn trill of the boatswain's mate's pipes piped the men to breakfast, and we descended to the steerage to get dressed.

By the time we had finished, "All hands!" was called, followed by, "Hands, up anchor!"

The same order was solemnly made known to us by the quartermaster of the watch, although the fact was patent to anyone by the rush and tramp of marines and bluejackets as they went to their stations. The anchor was weighed in those days by hand. Our lower, main, and upper deck capstans were all pinned together so as to work as one, and could be manned by at least five hundred men. With the exception of orders, all work on board the *Hero* was carried on in perfect silence, which was strictly enforced by our Commander. The word "Silence" appeared in all sorts of places, even in the tops; and on the ship's wheel, instead

of the usual patriotic motto, " Silence " shone
out in letters of gold.

The capstans were now fully manned, and
the officers at their stations. The Prince and
suite by this time were on the poop, interested
spectators of the animated scene. The Commander touched his cap to the Commodore, and
reported, " All ready, sir."

" Carry on, if you please, Captain Stirling,"
was the reply.

All other orders now came from the Commander.

" Bring to, below."

" Brought to, sir !" comes up in a few
minutes.

" Heave round !"

A trill of pipes, a few taps from the drums to
mark the time, and as the men at the three
great capstans swing into their stride, the fifes
and drums break out into a merry, brattling air,
to which the cable comes in in gallant style.

I noticed His Royal Highness came forward
to the break of the poop, to look down with an
amused smile at the brawny figures manning

the capstan-bars, and a fine sight they presented
to him as they stamped steadily round to the
music.

The various stages of the table were reported
from the knight-heads by the stentorian voice
of our First-Lieutenant, which might have been
heard at Cawsand Bay.

" Up and down, sir!" at which the cat and
fish falls were led along.   " Anchor away, sir!"

The Commodore approaches the engine-room
telegraph, and a few turns of the screw keeps
the ship in her place   The next minute,
" Heave and in sight! Clear anchor, sir!" comes
from for'ard, and " Avast heaving!" from the
Commander, followed by " Hook the cat!"

A wave of the hand from the First indicates
all right for'ard.

" Man the catfall!" is the order. " Haul
taut!" " Surge the cable!" followed by a
rumble from the lower-deck, " Away with the
cat!" and the great anchor comes merrily up to
the cathead.

By this time the *Hero* was gliding past the
royal yacht, on the paddle-box of which stood

DEPARTURE OF THE PRINCE OF WALES FROM PI.

the Prince Consort and suite, waving a farewell to the Prince, who walked aft to the taffrail to return his father's salute. The anchor is fixed and secured, the capstans unrigged, and we steam out of the western entrance of the Sound, followed by our consort, the *Ariadne*, the Prince's standard floating at our maintop-gallant masthead. A final flutter of farewell signals, and we head for the Channel Fleet, which is lying about six miles in the offing. The ships were in two columns, through which we were to pass.

It was just seven o'clock as we passed the breakwater; before eight o'clock we were close up to the fleet. They were under sail and steam, and presented a splendid sight. The fleet was composed of the *Royal Albert* (flagship), 120 guns; *Edgar* (flagship), 91 guns; *Aboukir*, 91 guns; *Algiers*, 91 guns; *Conqueror*, 101 guns; *Donegal*, 101 guns; *Centurion*, 80 guns; *Mars*, 80 guns; *Mersey*, 40 guns; *Diadem*, 32 guns; and *Greyhound*, 17 guns.

As we passed through the double column, each ship saluted and manned the rigging. We steamed on, and took our station at the head of the columns. As a fair wind was springing up, we also made all plain sail, and in a few hours the blue land faded into the distance, and we were at sea. A down-Channel course was shaped, and under steam and sail we were going eleven knots, which was considered a good speed in those days.

A word of explanation here as to steam-power in the navy at that time. Steam was only used on special occasions. The Admiralty regulations as to the use of steam were most stringent. I have been for ten days at a time walloping about on the Line in a frigate with her benches full of coal, dead calm, pitch boiling out of the seams, sails slattering themselves to pieces as the ship rolled, and the men harassed about to trim sails to every breath of air, when a few hours' steaming would have put us into the north-east trades. It was, in my day, seamanship first, gunnery second, and steam nowhere; now, in the navy, the two last are bracketed in a dead-heat, and seamanship, as it was understood then, not entered. To handle a ship under sail in all conditions of weather was the height of most officers' ambitions. These were, however, far-seeing men, who noted the signs of the times, and aimed at being something more than mere salt-horse officers. It was none too soon, and they got their reward.

To resume our voyage. The weather still continued fine and the water smooth, and the motion of the heavy line-of-battle ship so far did not seem to inconvenience our royal passenger, as he and most of the suite remained on deck watching the fleet. To keep station, a ship would shorten or make sail, and one or another of the ships were constantly clewing up their courses or topgallant sails, or making more sail. It appeared to interest His Royal Highness, the degree of smartness with which the ships worked. It was easy to notice the ships longest in commission.

The *Conqueror* at that time claimed to be the smartest ship. The following year she was lost at Rum Cay, in the Bahama Group, and I saw the whole of her ship's company, amounting to about 910 officers and men, tried by court-martial on board the *Hero* for the loss of their ship.

Towards evening we parted company with the fleet. The *Greyhound*, a smart 17-gun corvette, steamed up under our lee-quarter to take our final letters, as she was going into Plymouth. The sea was beginning to rise, and the smaller ship knocked about a good deal. She was also under sail, and hove-to about two cables' length from us. My boat, the first cutter, was called away. As myself and the boat's crew came up on the poop, His Royal Highness came forward and looked on as we scrambled along the davits and got into the boat; the mail-bag and a white leather despatch-bag were handed in. We had Clifford's patent lowering apparatus. It did not take long to lower us down to a safe height, from which we dropped with a slap into the water, and pulled over to the *Greyhound*. I scrambled on board with the bags, got the Commander's receipt for them; into the boat again, and, having got clear of the *Greyhound*, made for our ship. We had several duckings before we got alongside, hooked on, and were hoisted up, boat's crew and all, to our davits. A final farewell signal was made, the fleet hauled their wind to continue their cruise, and we were left to ourselves to pursue our voyage.

*   *   *   *   *

We were now well at sea, the wind on our port quarter, but with a tendency to veer round to the south, and squally. The ship was fairly steady, and dinner for the Prince and suite was served in the forecabin, the band discoursing a popular programme of music under the half-deck. There were no invitations issued that evening to the officers. That was an honour to come when we settled down and our illustrious passengers got their sea-legs. It would not do to risk the spectacle of His Royal Highness, or even one of the suite, suddenly rising from the table and making for his cabin with an unsteady lurch. Such a thing did happen once or twice, I was informed on good authority, but no one need be ashamed of being seasick, for is it not chronicled that our greatest sailor, Lord

Nelson, was always seasick when he went to sea? I used to try and make the thought console *me* when I leaned over the lee gangway and paid my tribute to Neptune, but somehow or other the consolation didn't come off.

We have got so far as to get the first royal dinner under way. So it is time now to give my impressions of the personal appearance of His Majesty nearly fifty years ago.

I shall certainly not be guilty of any flattery when I say that he was at that time an exceedingly handsome young man. There will be included amongst the illustrations an engraving of a medal in my possession, which was struck to commemorate his visit to Canada. The medal is engraved by Wyon, the chief engraver of His Majesty's seals, and gives His Royal Highness's profile. My readers can judge for themselves. The likeness is a capital one, as it ought to be, for I heard the Prince say at dinner one night, when someone mentioned the excellence of the work, that he sat no less than seventeen times before the designers were satisfied. His Royal Highness at that time was very like Her late Majesty in the early years of her reign. He had good hair, beautiful teeth, and a delicate complexion. His figure was slight, and he carried himself erect and gracefully. In fact, he looked the Prince all over. His manner to those who had the honour of being brought in contact with him was charming. In spite of his exalted rank, one felt at ease with him at once. He gave growing proof of the immense popularity which he enjoyed as he took his place in the nation's life. The Prince is now King, and I will venture to prophesy that His Majesty will be the most popular King that ever sat on the British throne.

Now for the suite. His Grace the Duke of Newcastle, our next passenger in order of precedence, although not in popularity, was a mighty noble, and looked it. He was a man slightly above middle height, with a cold blue eye and light reddish hair and beard, which last attracted a good deal of adverse notice, as it was unusual. The same beard came in one day for an amusing remark by Harry Graydon, the second Captain of my top, as we were aloft at some duty, which I will mention later on. The Duke stood a good deal aloof from everyone, and spent most of his time below with his private secretary. He usually came on deck when any evolution was being done, and looked on with a critical eye. He was a member of the Cabinet; perhaps he thought he would swap his billet of the Colonies for First Lord of the Admiralty, and was picking up a wrinkle or two in seamanship to astonish his colleagues when he took over the office of " Ruler of the Queen's Navee."

He gave one the impression of a man of extreme hauteur, and I was rather surprised, after the cruise was over, to receive a letter from him, beginning " Dear Mr. Gough," and enclosing a very handsome photograph of himself with his autograph on it, and a request for mine in return—a request " Dear Mr. Gough " complied with.

Then there was the Earl of St. Germans, the Lord Steward, really a most charming old gentleman, very aristocratic - looking. His manners were old-fashioned and stately, quite the manners of the Regency. He was an old man—I should think, over seventy—and it was a plucky thing for him to take a voyage across the Atlantic at his time of life; but he was a courtier of the first water, and the Queen's wish for him to accompany her royal son was to him above all personal discomfort. He was very fond of coming down on the quarter-deck to have a yarn with the midshipman of the watch, as the poop was too windy for him. He would hang on to anything handy while he talked; but sometimes he used to fetch away, and then the middy had to make a grab at him. If he had too much way on, then was seen the comical sight of a belted elderly Earl sliding across Her Majesty's quarter-deck with a light-weight midshipman hanging on to him as a brake. It ended with the two bringing up with a jerk against the first obstacle, when the midshipman would haul his lordship back again to a place of safety.

Dr. Acland was another passenger—a clever-looking man. We did not see much of him. I don't think his services were ever required, as His Royal Highness enjoyed the best of health. I noticed Dr. Acland's death in 1900 as Sir

8

H. W. Acland, Regius Professor of Medicine at Oxford.

Of the Prince's personal suite, the first was Major-General the Hon. Robert Bruce, governor to His Royal Highness. He was a very handsome, elderly man, with iron-grey hair and moustache, a trim, upright figure, clear-cut features, and a kindly twinkle in his eyes. He gave me the idea of a man with any amount of quiet tact. When in full uniform, he looked the very model of a modern Major-General (of the day); what his exact duties were as the Prince's governor I could not say. His Royal Highness was approaching manhood, and, I should think, could pretty well run himself; but I should imagine that General Bruce accompanied the Prince more as a friendly and reliable adviser, whose knowledge of men and the world in general was invaluable.

Of His Royal Highness's two equerries, Major Teesdale and Captain Grey, I must postpone any mention until a little later on. I was brought into personal contact with the first through some friends of mine, and I experienced the greatest kindness from him. So we will turn again to H.M.S. *Hero* and her progress.

The weather was beginning to change for the worse, the wind still veering round to the south and west. It was my first watch that night, and when I came on deck at eight o'clock it had every appearance of a dirty night. The wind was about abeam, coming in squalls. We were still under steam and sail. We had long ago furled the royals and sent the yards down. The Commodore was on deck, and looked rather anxious. He ordered the Lieutenant of my watch, Viscount Kilcoursie, before our watch was called, to reef topsails with both watches. The work was done with extra smartness by such a lot of men. As I have previously mentioned, Lord Kilcoursie was a first-class officer and seaman, and knew his duty. The topsail yards were down, two reefs taken in, and the yards up again under five minutes (although it was pitch-dark and blowing hard), the topgallant sails set above them, the watch was called, and we looked pretty snug for the night.

That first watch of mine saw the beginning of what I can safely say was the only blot on the whole of our cruise.

We had a gun-room steward, who was a first class steward in his way. I do not remember the man's name, although the events I am about to relate impressed themselves deeply on my mind. The gun-room mess was always well looked after by our steward. He had, however, one failing: he was a private soaker. He was never exactly drunk, but he was always quietly nipping, generally in our storeroom in the steerage.

About five bells (half-past ten) in the first watch I was walking up and down the quarter-deck. Everything was quiet. His lordship was pacing the break of the poop, alert and watchful. I had two other midshipmen on the quarter-deck with me, but they were having a quiet caulk—that is, a nap—under the weather hammock-nettings. The officers of the watch consisted of our noble Lieutenant, a mate on the forecastle (there were no Sub-lieutenants in those days), and three midshipmen on the quarter-deck. We used to divide the watch into three parts, and, if there was no duty going on, two of us would coil ourselves up in some sheltered nook and have a sleep. Of course, if the Commander came on deck, a quiet kick roused the sleepy mids, who sprang to their stations.

Lord Kilcoursie was a rattling good fellow, and never noticed that there was only one midshipman on the quarter-deck when there ought to have been three. He had been through the mill himself, and knew how sleepy boys always were.

As I said, everything was quiet for a ship at sea. There was the slap of the water as it struck the ship, the hum of the wind through the rigging rising to a low whistle as a squall came, the creak of the timbers, the guns and ladders, as the ship heeled over.

I was just turning round to commence my walk aft, thinking what a beastly long time it was before the ship's bell tolled out its next six strokes, dealt out by the marine sentry, who, I suppose, was equally glad to hear the strokes mounting up, when, as I turned, I saw a figure skulking among the lee quarter-deck guns. I walked over and called out:

"What man is that there? What are you doing there?"

The figure came forward, and I saw it was our gun-room steward. Addressing him by name, I asked him what he was doing there at that time of the night, and why he was not below in his hammock. He held up a warning hand, and began to speak in a frightened whisper.

"Oh, sir," he said, "will you go for'ard an' tell Mr. W. I want to see him?"

W. was the mate of our watch, and our wine-caterer.

"Why don't you go yourself?" said I.

"Oh no, no, sir," replied the steward.

"Why not?" I asked.

"I can't, sir. Don't you see them?" he said in a whisper.

"See who?" said I.

"Why, those rascals in the lee gangway," he replied, pointing to the gangway.

As a matter of fact, there was no one there at all.

I stared at the steward, if anyone could be said to stare in a dark night.

"Come over here, sir," he said. "I will tell you all about it."

I followed him over to the lee of the main-mast, and he there began to tell me an extra-ordinary yet probable story.

I might mention that no spirits are allowed in the gun-room mess—only "port, sherry, claret, and wine of that description," to quote the Admiralty regulation. Of course there was the daily ration of rum; that didn't count.

The steward's story was that W., our wine-caterer, had ordered some dozens of whisky, had them labelled as sherry and sent on board as part of our sea-stock; that some marines who were taking the case below broke one, and find-ing what the contents were, came to the steward and threatened to inform if they were not paid £50 by W.

"They came to me to-night, sir," said the steward, "and said time was up, and if they didn't get the money by nine o'clock to-morrow morning, they were going to split."

Now, this was a very serious thing; if true, it would perhaps mean W.'s loss of his commission. I went on to my sleeping watch-mates, and, giving one of them a shake, told him I had to go for'ard, and to get up and look after the quarter-deck. When I got on the forecastle, I found W. in his oilskins under the lee of the weather-hammock nettings. He was a very popular fellow in the mess, the son of an Admiral, and always addressed as "old" W. Why, I don't know, as he was a young man of twenty; but some men always are called "old-So-and-so."

"What do you want?" he said to me as I came for'ard.

"Look here, W.," said I, "our steward is aft and says he wants to see you at once."

"What about?"

"I think it is about that case the marines broke," I replied.

"The case the marines broke? What on earth are you talking about?"

"Don't you know about the case?" questioned I.

"No," said W., "and I'll be hanged if I know what you're driving at."

I repeated the steward's story.

"There's not a word of truth in the fellow's yarn. Why, he's mad, or got d.t.'s."

This was very strange, so I said nothing.

"Where is the fellow now?" asked W.

"I left him standing by the main hatchway when I came for'ard."

W. thought a minute or two.

"You had better come aft with me," said W. at last.

We came along the weather gangway, but when we got to the place where I had left the steward standing, he was nowhere to be seen.

"Send the ship's corporal of the watch to me, Gough."

I got the corporal, and W. told him to go below and try and find the steward, to get him into his hammock, to tell the nearest sentry to keep an eye on him, and to take him to the sick-bay in the morning.

After about a quarter of an hour the corporal returned, and reported that he had got the steward to his hammock, but that he was very shaky, and muttering to himself.

We went to our stations again, and the watch ended without further adventure. We were relieved, ·and turned into our hammocks thoroughly tired out with the long day's work, and so ended our first day at sea with His Royal Highness on board.

     *   *   *   *   *

The 11th of July saw H.M.S. *Hero* fighting her way in the teeth of a heavy gale. During the night the wind had veered round to south-west. In the morning watch we had furled sails, sent down the topgallant yards, housed topgallant masts, and pointed yards to the wind; we kept a little to the leeward of our course, that we might have the advantage of our fore-and-aft canvas, and we thrashed along, with the assistance of our fore and main trysails and storm staysails, at about six knots an hour. Although the *Hero* was 600 nominal horse-power, with our heavy top hamper, we could not have done much more than four knots if the ship had been kept head on to the wind. There was a nasty chopping sea, in which the ship pitched heavily; we were hardly clear of the Channel, and did not get the long roll of the Atlantic.

In the *Hero's* steerage, as we turned out, we got very evident proof of the state of the weather on deck. A midshipman has to make his toilet at his sea-chest by the aid of a ship's candle, commonly known in the service as a " purser's dip." In the middle of his operation the lid of the chest usually came down with an impresive slap, followed by an equally impressive oath from the owner. When he proceeded to prop it up again, he would probably be knocked up against his chest by an energetic mizzen-top-man as he worked backward like a crab with a wet swab in his fist. Another profane explosion, with " Beg parding, sur—didn't see you," from the topman. However, in those days a mid-shipman, once he started dressing when the ship was at sea, did not lose much time over it. In harbour it was different. An animated debate was generally carried on as to the merits of the girls performing at the "Blue Bells," or "how drunk old So-and-so was at 'The Keppel's Nut' last night," a well-known Portsmouth junior officers' hostelry of those days, the proper name being "The Keppel's Head."

On this particular morning, as we made our way to the gun-room, the state of the lower-deck gave further proof of the weather. The lower-deck ports were barred in, mess traps knocking about, guns and carriages creaking and straining, while with 800 odd men berthed on the deck, the atmosphere had a fine bad taste. There is an old saying in the service that "God might turn a midshipman's heart, but He could not turn his stomach," and it certainly would be believed if anyone saw the breakfast a midshipman could put away under such circumstances.

The gun-room steward did not appear, and W. asked the second steward about him. The answer was that he was on the sick-list. W. did not seem inclined to talk about our experience of the previous night, and of course I followed his lead. Breakfast in the gun-room had to be over at one bell (half-past eight), when we had to go to our quarters, "clean guns and arms."

As the weather was so bad, the men at the upper-deck quarters were ordered to clean their arms on the main-deck. When I was with them, I heard woeful sounds coming from the palace servants' cabins, and I wondered how old "Twenty Stun" and his fellows were getting along. They were evidently having a pretty rough time of it, judging by the various noises that came from behind the bulkheads.

At two bells (nine o'clock) the drums beat to quarters for inspection, and the men fell in in rear of their guns, when they were inspected by their respective Lieutenants.

As I previously mentioned, I was midshipman of the quarter-deck quarters, so saw everything that was going on on deck. None of our passengers made an appearance except Major Teesdale and Captain Grey. The former was an old campaigner, and did not seem to mind the weather, whilst the latter was an accomplished yachtsman, and had won his sea-legs. The two soldiers looked on at the inspection going

9

on on the quarter-deck, evidently amused at the wonderful way the bluejackets kept their formation as the First-Lieutenant walked round, inspecting their rifles and cutlasses, followed by myself, note-book in pocket, ready to put down any unfortunate wight's name whose arms or clothing were dirty. Our inspection was always over first, and we had to wait until the other Lieutenants came up from the lower and main decks and made their reports. In the interval I was regarding Major Teesdale with a good deal of youthful veneration. A Victoria Cross man was something to be looked upon with enthusiasm, and this one in particular; we had heard such wonderful stories of his heroism.

At length the last report was made to the Commander, who in turn reported the whole to the Commodore. The retreat was beaten, the men dismissed, and we were free to go.

As I was about to go down the quarter-deck ladder, I heard " Mr. Gough " from the Commodore. Of course I was up the poop-ladder like a lamp-lighter, and, standing before him, " Sir," I said, hand to cap.

"Oh," he said, "Major Teesdale wants to see you."

Another touch of the cap, and I walked aft to where the Major was standing, looking at our consort, who was steadily keeping station. He had his back to me as I approached, so I said, "Do you want me, sir?"

He faced round, and said, "Oh, you are Mr. Gough! How do you do?" with a smile, holding out his hand. "Do you know," he went on, "I have been told to look after you?"

Seeing I looked puzzled, he said:

"General Bloomfield is a connection of yours, is he not?"

The old gentleman in question was a relative of my mother's. I explained our relationship.

"Well," continued the Major, "I was on his staff for some time. I met him the other day in London, and when he knew I was coming out in the *Hero* with the Prince, he asked me to have a look after you. But," he went on, with a hearty laugh, "I think it's the other way about, and you will have to look after me, especially if you are going to have such weather as this."

He quite won me over by his frank manner and pleasant style.

The Major was a very handsome fellow—a well-knit, soldierly figure, fair hair, and trim moustache, which he always wore smartly pointed. The most notable feature about him were his eyes. They were blue, with a curious daring, steely glint in them. I have never seen eyes like them since, except once, and they belonged to a fair, blue-eyed Spaniard I knew in South America.

Major Teesdale had won his V.C. by his gallant conduct at the Siege of Kars, under Sir Fenwick Williams, where he commanded in an advanced redoubt. He rallied the Turks, drove out the Russians by a brilliant charge, and turned the fortunes of the day. He combined valour with humanity, as, when the Turks drove back the Russians and they proceeded to bayonet the wounded, Major Teesdale saved the unfortunate men from being massacred.

The act was witnessed by the Russian General Mouravieff, who gratefully acknowledged it before his staff. The Major was also a C.B., Knight of the Legion of Honour, and Mejidie of the third class.

Such was the record of the man I stood talking to, and I think my readers will allow that it was enough to call for the boyish admiration with which I regarded him. The Crimean War was still fresh in our memories in those days. It had been brought vividly direct to me by the loss of a near relative in the final assault on the Redan, my father's brother, Colonel Thomas Bunbury Gough, and I had messmates who were participants in the great struggle. The Indian Mutiny was also beginning to pour its heroes home fresh from " deeds that won the Empire," so young fellows in both services had no lack of incentive to fame.

Major Teesdale said he would be happy to be of service to me in any way during the Prince's tour, and went on to say that he knew others of my people, also V.C. men.

10

"I hope you will make as good a sailor as they are soldiers," he said kindly. "The Commander tells me you are a very smart young fellow, and will make a good officer."

I thought this was very good of the Commander, and if I stood so well with him, perhaps I could knock some more leave out of him when we got to Canada. I had had mighty little of it from him; it was always, "What do you want to go on shore for? Stay on board and learn your duty."

"Do you know my brother-equerry, Grey?" asked the Major. "Come over, and I'll introduce you." And we went across the poop. "Grey," he continued, "this is young Gough of whom I spoke."

Captain Grey turned round and held out his hand.

As I shook hands with the stalwart Guardsman I felt I had two good friends in the men beside me, and so I had; they were always doing kind little things for the youngsters. Captain Grey was a fine-looking man, wearing long Dundreary whiskers and moustache, which was the fashion at that time. After a few minutes' more conversation, the two soldiers descended to look after some breakfast, and I went to the gun-room. The atmosphere on the lower-deck was a little sweeter: several wind-sails had been got up, and the watch on deck had relieved the breathing-space. The gale still kept on, the ship straining and pitching in the short seas, and it was a bad time for most of our passengers, from His Royal Highness down to the palace retainers.

It was my afternoon watch that day, and when I came on deck the weather showed no sign of mending, there was more sea on, and the old ship was pitching into it all she knew, one moment pointing her jib-boom up as if she was trying to stab the low clouds, and then making a downward plunge, throwing half the screw out of water. They were good ones to pitch, were the screw line-of-battle ships of that time. They could do a bit of rolling, too, when it suited them. I have seen the *Hero* dip her quarter-boats every roll when running before a gale. I do not think that I ever saw her pitching so heavily as on this occasion. Ships are curious things, and seem to take it into their heads to behave badly at times. At four bells, when I went on the poop to heave the log, I remember looking for'ard, and noticing that at times I could see the horizon above the foreyard as the ship took her downward plunge. I wondered how His Royal Highness felt immediately below me: the sensation right aft was as if you had left something inside you behind as the stern lifted. I heard afterwards that the Prince had got through the gale fairly well, and took the knocking about he got with his invariable good-humour. I found the ship was making only four knots, and reported the speed to Lord Kilcoursie, who told me to log it. I went down on the main-deck to enter it up in the rough log. As I was going up the quarter-deck ladder on my return, I felt someone touch me on the shoulder. I turned round, hanging on to the man-rope, and saw the gun-room steward, who was holding on tight to a stanchion. The man presented a pitiable aspect. His face was deadly white, his features twitching, and there was a mad glare in his eyes, which thoroughly alarmed me for him.

" For God's sake, sir," he said, " tell Mr. W. I want him."

I addressed him by name, saying that I thought he was on the sick-list, and telling him that he ought to be below, but he maintained he was all right: he only wanted Mr. W. for a moment. He kept repeating this. I said that matters were not as bad as he told me last night, and, to quiet him, said I would see Mr. W. for him as soon I got on deck. He seemed to be easier when I told him this; but before I went up the ladder I told the marine sentry to keep an eye on the man, as he was sick. I determined to go for'ard and see W.: he was a mate, and his experience and standing was of weight—he could advise what was best to be done for the unfortunate steward. When I got on the forecastle, I found W. looking after some of the gunners' crew, who were tauting up the securing-chains of the big pivot-guns, which had worked loose. I called him to one side to tell him about the condition of the steward.

"Why," said W., "I thought the man was on the sick-list. He has got a bad attack of d.t.'s, and is as mad as a March hare; he ought to be under restraint."

"What am I to do about him?" I questioned.

"You see, I can't leave the forecastle, Gough. But go and get the ship's corporal of the watch; tell him of the man's condition; also tell him to take him to the sick-bay at once, and send for one of the doctors."

Just as I was turning to follow out W.'s directions, we heard a most diabolical yell from the fore hatchway, and the next moment the steward burst up it, glared round for a moment, and the next instant, before anyone could divine his intentions, made a run to the ship's side, clambered on to the hammock-netting, and with another yell jumped clean overboard.

Man overboard!" shouted W. at the top of his powerful voice.

I sped along the weather gangway, repeating the alarm.

"Lifeboat's crew away!" I sang out to the boatswain's mate. But the boat's crew had already heard the call, and were streaming up the main hatchway, and well on their way to the boat's davits. Everything was done with promptitude. Lord Kilcoursie had rushed to the engine-room telegraph and stopped the engines. As I came up the poop-ladder I had run to the davits to get into the boat. He ordered me back, and told me to go up the mizzen rigging and keep a lookout for the man, he going into the boat himself.

By this time the Commodore and Commander were both on deck, with many of the officers. The ship was brought head to the wind. I never saw a smarter piece of work in the navy than the lowering of that boat. Almost before the ship's way had been stopped she was down safely and away.

In the meantime I had my eye on the man, whose head I could see at times as he rose on the seas. He was close to the lifebuoy, which had been promptly let go. I was assisted by our sailing-master, who directed the signalman

standing on the spanker-boom which direction
he was to signal for our boat to pull. As the
boat came up to the steward, he was swimming
strongly, but made no effort to make for the
lifebuoy. On approaching closer, the unfortunate fellow gave another wild yell, threw up his
arms, and sank slowly. The boat pulled about
for over a quarter of an hour, but there was no
further appearance of the man, and the boat was
recalled. In the meantime, our consort, the
Ariadne, had also a boat ready to lower; but
they evidently thought we had succeeded in
rescuing the steward, and did not send her.
We had some difficulty in picking up our boat;
but once she was hooked _on, she was quickly
run up to the davits and secured.

The loss of the steward was the only blot on
our cruise. An inquiry was held as to why the
man was not on the sick-list and put under
restraint. The blame—if any—lay on the sick-
bay steward for not reporting his condition to
our surgeon; but he explained that the man
spoke to him quite rationally, and said he was
not sick, and the inquiry ended with no more

result than the sick-bay man being told to be more careful in future.

I do not think our royal passenger learnt the facts of the case until some days afterwards. The Commodore did not want His Royal Highness to be shocked at the tragic end of the unfortunate fellow. That a man was lost overboard he must have known at the time, but I do not think that he knew that the steward destroyed himself. To end up the matter, on examining the storeroom, proof was found that there was something in his story about the whisky being on board, as two cases—less what he had drunk himself—were found. He had evidently got them on board by some means. They were sealed up and struck into the spiritroom.

That evening the wind began to drop, and about nine o'clock there was only a strong breeze blowing. It was a summer's gale, which had evidently blown itself out, and there was every prospect of finer weather. In the middle watch we were doing our nine knots under steam, with the wind still dropping

The 12th of July found the *Hero* steaming direct on her course for St. John's, Newfoundland, the first port which the Prince was to visit. All traces of the late gale had disappeared, with the exception of a heavy swell rolling in from the south-west; the long roll of the Atlantic did not interfere with the ship's steaming power like the short, choppy seas of the Channel. There was very little wind, and the sun shone brightly; the men were employed in a general clean-up, and in the afternoon no one could have imagined that the trim, well-ordered man-o'-war was the same storm-beaten ship of the day before. But a well-directed ship's company can work wonders in a few hours, and when the Prince made his first appearance on deck, everything was as spick and span as a new pin. His Royal Highness had evidently got his sea-legs, and paced the poop with the Commodore like a regular sea-dog. He took a great deal of interest in all the little details of the routine carried on, from the midshipman of the watch heaving the log to the relief of the wheels. Signals of inquiry as to the welfare of our illustrious freight were being made by the *Ariadne*, the replies to which were dictated by the Prince; and the smartness with which the various flags were sorted from the signal-lockers by the signalmen, the rapidity with which they were bent on, hoisted, and answered (there were no semaphores in the service then), all seemed to amuse His Royal Highness. Everyone was glad to see him so hearty and jolly, and I am certain that he had a good appetite for lunch after his morning's blow on the poop. Several others of our passengers were also on deck. Lord St. Germans came up and enjoyed the sunshine. The old gentleman expressed his thanks in courteous terms to anyone who offered him an arm to move about—in fact, it was quite a pleasure to be thanked by him. I assisted him down the poop-ladder, and was thanked as if I had rendered him some signal service instead of doing what I had always been taught to do, and what every boy ought, and that is, to assist an old man in difficulties. His lordship became a prime favourite with everyone on board, and we were always ready to do anything for his comfort.

The Duke of Newcastle did not appear in the forenoon; I presume he was engaged in cares of State; he came up later on in the day. The palace retainers also were beginning to get about, but not on deck; that was what some of us looked forward to with a view to future fun, which came in due course.

In the meantime the *Hero* was steadily steaming along, but anxious glances were cast from time to time by the Commodore, Commander, and master for any sign of a fair wind. We were certainly not going to make the passage out under steam, and advantage was to be taken of every slant of wind. Luck seemed to be in our favour. In the afternoon a good breeze from the south-east began to spring up, the engines were stopped, sail made on the ship, the screw disconnected and hoisted, and we exchanged the thump, thump, thump of the steamer for the easy glide and roll of a sailing-ship with a fair wind. The *Hero* was always a good sailer. All belonging to her were glad of the change, which was also acceptable to our passengers.

That evening, when the men were at quarters, there was a strong muster of interested spectators on the poop; H.R.H. the Prince, the Duke of Newcastle, Lord St. Germans, Dr. Acland—in fact, all His Royal Highness's party were on deck enjoying the fine breeze. After quarters we reefed topsails, a practice generally then followed out in the service when making a passage. It made the ship snugger for the night, and saved trouble during the watches. A man-o'-war at that time was not a clipper trying to break the record, but jogged along with a due regard to spars and sails.

I have mentioned in a previous chapter one of the second Captains of the maintop, by name Harry Graydon. There were two second Captains of each top, one in each watch.

Graydon was in the starboard watch. He was, to my mind, the very beau-ideal of a British man-of-war's-man. He had constituted himself a sort of aerial guardian of me when aloft, and I was mutually attracted to him. He was the type of man to attract one—a very good-looking fellow, tall, dark chestnut hair, handsome brown

11

eyes, always neat in his dress, respectful in his manner, and never presuming above his rank in life. Of all the thousands of seamen that I was shipmates with in the navy, Harry Graydon stands out as the foremost. Perhaps it was what I will relate a little farther on that brings his name and figure so vividly to my recollection. Graydon was a prime seaman, and many a knot and splice he taught me.

As I have said, we reefed topsails after evening quarters. It was usual in the *Hero* for the top midshipmen, the Captain of the top, and second Captains to remain up after the general order was given of " Down from aloft!" This was done that the petty officers might coil down ropes, see all gear clear for running, and generally put things to rights. The maintop of a line-of-battle ship of that date was as large as a good-sized room, perhaps sixteen feet or more athwartship by nearly as much fore and aft, and a lot of gear led into it.

On this particular evening we were waiting for the final order, " Clear tops!" which would have brought us down. The delay was caused by His Royal Highness engaging in conversation with the Commodore and Commander. My topmate, a mid by the name of T., whom I afterwards met in Melbourne, and myself stood looking down on deck. Behind us the three petty officers were also engaged in surveying the distinguished group on the poop. I turned round for a moment, and saw that Graydon evidently wanted to speak to me. He was too well trained to speak to an officer without first being spoken to.

" What is it, Graydon ?" I said.

" Beg pardon, sir," he said, touching his cap, " but "—I forget the other man's name, but we will call him Bill Jones—" Bill Jones and me would like to know the names of the toffs. Of course," he went on, " we knows the Prince, but if you would tell us the other gentlemen's names, we would take it very kind."

" Of course, Graydon," said I. " That tall gentleman with the beard is the Duke of New-castle, the old gentleman is Lord St. Germans ' and so on, as I gave him all their names.

" The Dook of Noocastle ! The Dook of

Noocastle!" repeated Graydon, looking at me with a dubious scratch of his head, and then at Bill Jones, who said:

"There! I told you so, Harry, you old fool!"

Graydon did not say anything for a moment or two, and then, approaching me closer, said, with another touch of his cap, but speaking in a confidential whisper:

"Beg pardon, sir. Is he a Rooshian?"

"What?"

"Why, sir," returned Graydon, "the gent with the beard."

"A Russian!" I replied; "I tell you he's an English Duke—the Duke of Newcastle."

"A Hinglish Dook is he, sir?" said Graydon, still speaking low, as if the object of his conversation was close alongside. "Then why does he wear a beard?" with an air of un-answerable argument.

Both my messmate and myself roared with laughter at Graydon's remarks, and even then he did not seem convinced.

"You see, sir," he said, "I was up the Black Sea—saw plenty of Rooshians up there;

they all had beards, every Jack man of them; so
had we, for the matter of that, when we was in
the trenches, but as soon as we got a bit of soap
and water we shaved ours off, while they kept
theirs on, the dirty beggars! It beats me why
a Hinglish Dook likes to wear a beard like a
dirty Rooshian."

Just then a sharp order, "Clear tops!" rang
out from below.

"There you are, Graydon," laughed I; "get
down from aloft!"

As he got outside the topmast rigging,
preparatory to descending the futtock shrouds,
he hung on for a moment, to fire a parting shot
at the object of his dislike.

"Don't you think, sir," he said, "that the
Prince ought to give the Dook a 'int to clear
that 'air off 'is face before he lands?" and he
disappeared below the top rim.

Poor Harry Graydon! When he came home
again, he married a pretty West-Country girl.
I remember his bringing her on board one
Sunday and showing her round the ship,
evidently as proud of her as she was of her

12

handsome husband. I happened to pass them
on the main-deck, and heard him say to her in
a stage-whisper that I was one of the midshipmen of his top; to which she replied, also in a
stage-whisper, that " I was a nice-looking young
gentleman." Being a very bashful boy, I
rapidly made sail in another quarter. I believe
I was a nice-looking boy in those days—very
unlike the bald-headed old buffer I now am!

Poor Graydon met his end in a subsequent
part of the *Hero's* commission—going out to
Bermuda—by being thrown from the maintop
sail-yard on deck and killed instantaneously.
He was the victim of his own daring; he used
to turn out on the yard holding on to the topgallant stunsail boom; the ship gave a send
for'ard, and he was thrown off the yard. He
fell across the gunwale of one of the boom
boats, and never spoke again. We buried him
at sea next day. As his messmates carried his
still form to the gangway, shrouded in the flag
under which he had fought, and the chaplain
read the Burial Service, I thought of the merry
laughing eyes and curly chestnut hair of my

humble friend, and of the poor girl in her little cottage in Plymouth waiting for the home-coming which never came. I was a soft-hearted young lubber in those days.

But to return to the *Hero*. That evening the first dinner-party was given by the Commodore. About eight officers were invited, four from the ward-room and four from the gun-room. I had not the honour of that night, but my turn came in due course, and we will leave the old ship spanking along with the wind on her port quarter and the beautiful music of our band throbbing along the decks, with all hands delighted at the prospect of making a good run across the Atlantic.

CHAPTER V

The *Ariadne* comes to close quarters—" Twenty Stun " and
the lackeys are taught manners.

THE fair wind which had favoured the *Hero*
continued, and next day saw us bowling along
about ten knots. There was not much sea on,
and the motion of the ship did not now inconvenience any of our passengers. The Prince
usually came on deck quite early, and the
midshipman of the watch was always sure of a
kindly greeting from His Royal Highness
before he ascended the poop-ladder. Once on
the poop, he would pace up and down with the
officer of the watch. The conversation must
generally have been of an amusing character,
judging from the bursts of laughter that were
heard on the quarter-deck. The Prince was
bubbling over with fun and good-nature, and
I am certain would have been glad of a jolly

good frolic with us boys, if there had been no chance of startling the proprieties in the shape of the Duke of Newcastle and General Bruce. The midshipmen all became boy courtiers. My friend Major Teesdale put me up to the etiquette necessary. When His Royal Highness addressed one of us, we were told not to make use of too many "His Royal Highnesses"; perhaps only one, after that " Sir." I passed the word on to my messmates, and there were no awkward mistakes. The Prince put everyone at once at their ease by his charming manner and kindly smile.

We had now been three days at sea, and had not sighted more than two or three ships. We had been keeping a more northerly course than ships take usually bound for America, whose ports are mostly New York or Boston. His Royal Highness expressed a wish to see a ship at sea under sail at close quarters. With a view to allow his wish to be gratified, the Commodore signalled to the *Ariadne* to close within speaking distance. At the same time, we hauled up our courses, let fly topgallant and royal sheets, and hauled down the flying-jib. As the ship's way was checked, our consort came up on our lee quarter, and His Royal Highness was presented with what I maintain is one of the finest sights in the world—that is, a ship at sea under full sail.

It was a superb thing to show the Prince. As the beautiful frigate came ranging up she lifted to the sea. Her copper shone like burnished gold; above, the long line of guns; aloft, her taut masts and rigging, her cloud of white canvas as steady as if carved; while above all her long blue pendant soared and flickered upward like a tongue of blue flame. I think, at that moment, His Royal Highness must have felt a glow of pride at the thought of being the first of all Englishmen, or, rather, say Britons. Boy-like, at first he uttered exclamations of delight, then his upturned face grew thoughtful; I wondered of what he was thinking. Did he realize his destiny? I had curious thoughts myself.

That eager, graceful, handsome boy, that beautiful frigate, a living thing circling like some great snow-bird on the leaden-grey of the Atlantic rollers because of a wish expressed by him! What a picture it was—the tea-lead sea, the royal pendant, a tongue of blue flame beneath a grey-blue sky, that great ship curtseying to please a Queen's son, and the streaming pendant, the royal boy! Fitting emblems all of Britain's greatness: the frigate of her sea-power, the pendant of her history, the boy of the loving loyalty of the people. I could have dared anything. I understood what it was to be British-born—to be loyal to a King. I could have died for him, and yet—nothing that I have put down exactly expresses what I felt.

The Commodore was evidently nervous as the *Ariadne* sailed close, but there was nothing to be nervous about—at least, from the *Ariadne*, handled as she was by the consummate seaman who commanded her. As she came still closer up, we could see the tall form of Captain Vansittart standing on the weather side of the bridge, cap in hand, as he bowed, gentleman and loyal subject as he was, to his future

Sovereign. A few inquiries were made by him as to the welfare of the Prince, which were answered by the Commodore. The signal to resume station was given, the *Hero* made sail again, whilst the *Ariadne* dropped astern to her usual distance.

Everything had now shaken down to the clockwork routine of a well-disciplined man-o'-war, with one exception : that was, the education of the numerous servants to the parts of the ship open to them and those closed to them. On board a man-o'-war there are well-defined differences as to places reserved for the various ranks. For instance, spaces are allowed to the ward-room and gun-room officers to smoke in ; the same distinctions are carried out in all the little customs of the Navy which go to make up a great whole. They are impressed on every boy's mind from the moment of joining, and become a part of his life. The unwritten law of tradition is handed down from century to century. It was with feelings of indignation that we saw the most sacred customs of the service broken in all directions by the servants.

They had a very handsome mess-room fitted up on the main-deck, and a space was allotted to them to smoke in if they chose to indulge in a cigar, a luxury provided for them, but they used to frequent the ward-room smoking-space. The principal offender, in our eyes, was old "Twenty Stun." He would dump himself down in all sorts of places, and in a few minutes a group of his fellow-servants would gather round him and discuss things generally. From his standing in the service of the palace he appeared to be looked up to as head of the gang. Of course he did not know any better, but the midshipmen did not consider that.

Who was going to tell the servants that they were breaking well-known rules? The Prince's messman, Mr. Parkes, was approached on the subject, and when he gave them a gentle hint about matters, was loftily told to mind his own business, which was to feed them. We tried various dodges to give them a shake-up, but they all failed.

It came to my turn to bring them to a proper state of mind, and in a rather rough manner,

too.   It was the afternoon watch ; the ship was
still under sail, but the wind was getting light.
I was keeping my watch on the lee side of the
quarter-deck with my watch-mates, when we saw
old "Twenty Stun" leisurely ascend the
quarter-deck ladder, followed by two or three
more flunkies.   He gave a good look round,
and then waddled along the weather side, taking
up a position near the capstan, where he held
forth on some grievance to the others.

Now, the weather side of the quarter-deck of
a man-o'-war is the holy of holies.   It is
reserved for the Captain, Commander, and com-
missioned officers.   In the old days it was even
more.   From the weather side of the quarter-
deck Nelson, Jervis, Collingwood, Howe, all
the great seamen of the past, fought their ships
and fleets.   It was on the supposed weather
side of the quarter-deck of the *Victory* that
Nelson fell—I say supposed, as the *Victory*
was dead before the wind when she approached
the enemy.

It was with feelings of disgust that we saw
the place of honour taken up by old " Twenty

Stun" and his companions, and many a glance
of scorn was directed from the lee side up to
windward whilst they gabbled away, innocent
that they were infringing a time-honoured
custom of the service. It was a fine afternoon.
Very few of the men were on deck. The watch
were sprawling about on the main-deck and
forecastle. All our passengers were below.
We cast appealing looks for sympathy to his
lordship of Kilcoursie on the break of the
poop. He, too, surveyed the group with amusement expressed in his eyes, and appeared to take
in the situation. He gave a glance aloft, then
looked at the compass, and gave another glance
at the dog-vane. I saw an almost imperceptible
move of the telescope, which brought me aft in
anticipation of an order. It came at once.

"Mr. Gough, watch and idlers, trim sails!"

"Ay, ay, sir!" sings out Mr. Gough.

"Boatswain's mate, watch and idlers, trim
sails!"

"Ay, ay, sir!" returns the boatswain's mate.
"Whew! Whittle! Whew!" goes the pipe.
"Watch and idlers, trim sails!" bawls he down

the main hatchway. "Tumble up, there, the watch and idlers!"

A rush of feet up the hatchways, and the deck is alive with men. The Captain of the afterguard makes a run at the main bitts, and throws out the heavy coils of the fore-brace ready for the men to pick up.

"Weather braces!" comes from the poop.

Old "Twenty Stun" and his companions are staring round them with astonishment. The men are evidently going to have a lark with them.

"All ready for'ard, sir!" comes from the forecastle, followed by "Haul taut! round in!" from the poop; and away gallop the men at the braces.

Old "Twenty Stun," with his following, have men in front of them, in rear, and on both sides.

Exclamations of remonstrance came from them. "Hallo! mind where you're shoving! Don't be rude, young man. Mind my toes, I say!"

Broad grins were on the faces of the Jacks

as they hustled and bustled the flunkeys in all directions.

"Hoo! hoo! hah!" gasped poor old "Twenty Stun," as a marine took him in the ribs and knocked the wind out of him. "O Lor'! I say, there, look out!"

He made a grab at another man, but missed, and next moment there was a tremendous whack, wallop! and down he came on the broad of his back. Another flunkey was also sprawling about the deck, and a third had taken the precaution to throw his arms in an affectionate embrace round one of the afterguard, and hung on to that place of safety.

In the meantime the men continued to enjoy the fun, and pranced about the deck in all directions, until the order, "Belay, the weather braces!" came from the poop. Even then the fellows did not stop their horse-play. I had been a satisfied spectator of the proceedings, but I thought it time to interfere.

"What the d——l are you men about?" said I, as I came forward with a well-assumed air of

13

solicitude. "Pick those people up at once," I ordered.

The men obeyed, still grinning, but poor old "Twenty Stun" had to be propped up against the capstan to recover himself. He gasped and gasped, as he got his wind.

"How do you feel now?" asked I. "Here, get him a drink of water," I continued to one of the men.

After a drink, the old fellow was assisted to his feet, and I told two of the men to get him below. He was evidently astonished at the authority a boy like myself exercised; but a midshipman is a great man in a small way at times, and that is when everyone present is below him in rank, and none above him.

About half an hour afterwards I saw him on the main-deck. He came up to me. "I'm werry much obliged to you, sir," he said. "It was werry kind of you getting them men off; they're werry rough indeed."

"Well, I am glad to see you are all right; but it would not have happened if you had not been where you had no business to be."

" No business, sir ?" he asked, opening his eyes very wide.

" Yes," I returned, and went on to explain to him the different parts of the ship that were not to be made common use of.

" I'm werry grateful to you, sir," the old fellow said. " I'll take care and let the others know, and none of them will go near them places. But, Lor', them men of yours are werry rough."

We had no more trouble from the flunkeys after the rough lesson they got. The old man evidently put them in their place, for we afterwards had many a yarn with old " Twenty Stun," and found him not half a bad old fellow— in fact, the other way about—a jolly good sort. He was full of anecdotes about the palace, which were most amusing, and extended over twenty-seven years. He commènced as page to King William IV.

CHAPTER VI

Dining with the Prince—His Royal Highness lands at
St. John's, Newfoundland—Festivities on shore.

THE wind that had given the *Hero* a good start
on her voyage now dropped, and we had to get
up steam again, but we had run a good distance, and any fears that our coal-supply would
give out were dispelled. I remember the
laughter that was occasioned by the accounts
we read in the home papers, in which our voyage
was described as tempestuous. As far as I can
recollect, with the exception of the first blow
that we encountered in the chops of the Channel,
we had ordinary Atlantic summer weather, with
varying winds—sometimes in our favour, when
we made sail, at other times too light to be of
service, or against us, when we proceeded under
steam. As we got to mid-Atlantic a sharp lookout was kept for ice. The temperature of the

sea-water was taken every hour during the day, and half-hourly at night. We took no chance, with the heir-apparent to the throne of Great Britain on board. We saw no ice, but one night we must have been in close proximity to it, as the temperature dropped 20° in an hour; extra lookouts were posted and every precaution taken, but in the morning nothing was in sight.

The usual routine was carried out. On Sunday divine service was performed on the main-deck, which the Prince and all his suite attended.

A few days after we got to sea I had the honour of an invitation to dinner in the cabin. At seven o'clock the invited officers, to the number of eight, were ushered into the after-cabin. As we came forward the Prince advanced and shook hands with each officer, at the same time making some kindly remark. I used to think it curious how he knew all our names and duties, but he did. I believe it has developed into a wonderful gift, the remembrance of faces and names by His present Majesty. As soon as all the invited officers and suite were present,

14

the door was thrown open by Mr. Parkes, the Prince's messman, who announced, "Your Royal Highness, dinner is served." The Commodore led the way, followed by the Prince, the Duke, Earl, General, and the officers according to seniority, the rear being brought up by the two equerries. As the mids present were next to them, we got a nudge or two, with a whispered hope that we were hungry (which we were, of course), and what was going in the gun-room for dinner—"Any salt horse yet?" etc.

The table was laid athwartship in the fore-cabin. His Royal Highness sat in the centre of the table, the Duke of Newcastle on his right, the Commodore on his left; opposite to the Prince, the Earl of St. Germans; whilst the two ends of the table were occupied by the equerries. As we filed into the forecabin the band on the main-deck struck up "The Roast Beef of Old England," and in a few seconds we were all seated. The portly Mr. Parkes stood behind His Royal Highness, and personally attended to him. The rest of the guests were served by the Commodore's stewards, assisted by half a dozen of the servants in their gorgeous liveries, amongst whom old "Twenty Stun" was first. They were now quite as much at home as the stewards. I saw the old boy giving a fatherly glance at me now and then to see if I was getting on all right, and so I was. You may trust a midshipman to look after himself at dinner, even in the presence of royalty. The sight was really an impressive one. The long table glittering with its handsome appointments, the uniforms of the officers, from the epaulettes of the Commodore to the modest white turnback of the midshipmen, the soft music of the band from the main-deck, the four grim breeches of the cabin guns, completed a whole that must have impressed itself on the minds of those present. I know that it did on mine. The Prince and suite, with the exception of the two equerries, who were in uniform, appeared in simple evening dress. The dinners were always enjoyable. The affability of the Prince put aside all feeling of restraint. He generally addressed a few minutes' conversation to each officer present. Everything was bright and merry. After dinner coffee and cigars were served in the aftercabin, a brief interval of conversation, and the party broke up, the officers bowing to His Royal Highness and retiring.

I had many such dinners in the cabin. The gun-room officers entertained the Prince at dinner on the homeward voyage, which will be mentioned in due course. Our dinner, however, was not broken up voluntarily, and I will guarantee it was the wettest dinner His Majesty King Edward VII. ever had or is likely to have.

We were making steady progress across, and hoped to sight St. John's in a few days. We had been out now about eight days. I had some further experiences of old "Twenty Stun." He took a great interest in the ship's position, and would come up to me and yarn away; at times his conversation was most amusing. He could not say "v"—always used to pronounce it "w"—yet, strange to say, he was a Cockney. He generally commenced with, "Well, Mr. Gough, and 'ow are we getting on, sir?"

I'd explain to him our position, at which he'd

express his satisfaction by saying he was "werry glad to 'ear it."

One day I had a long yarn with him. The ship's fare evidently did not meet with his approval. He started by saying, "That Mr. Parkes, sir, is a werry 'aughty man, sir—werry 'aughty."

"Indeed," I asked, "what has he been doing?"

"Why, you see, sir," said the old fellow, "the other day there was a cold round of spiced beef put on our table—twice, sir, twice. So I says to him, 'Mr. Parkes, there's been a cold round of beef put on our table twice; see it don't occur again.' Will you believe me, sir, he took no notice of me?"

I laughed at the thought that if the spiced round of beef had been put on the gun-room table, there would not have been much chance of it coming on twice.

"Yes, sir," went on old "Twenty Stun," "that's what he did."

"I thought that they fed you very well."

"Feed!" said he, with a look of ineffable disgust—"feed, sir, why it's 'orrible! There

was a box of cigars sent in the other day—
Hawannas,' he calls them. Hawannas," he
repeated. "Cabbages, I calls them!"

"That's very bad," said I.

"But there's much wuss, sir—much wuss,"
said the old boy, shaking his head.

"I am sorry for that," I remarked.

"Yes," he went on, sinking his voice. "Why,
the wine that man Parkes gives us is reg'lar
undrinkable   The other day, when he sent in
some port, I says to him: 'Mr. Parkes, what
class of port do you call that?' He says: 'I
paid ninety-six shillings a dozen for it.' Will
you believe me, sir," he went on with increasing
solemnity, "'ere I've been twenty-seven years
in the palace, and I've never drunk wine under
ten shillings a bottle, and that was werry
inferior quality—werry inferior quality," he repeated, shaking his head.

I consoled him by telling him that he would
be at St. John's in a few days, and that he
could get some first-class port there, which is a
fact, or, rather, was.

"I 'ope so, sir," he remarked—"I 'ope so."

The old fellow's taste must have been very hard to please, as it happened we had some of the same wine in our mess, and grand stuff it was ; but wine at eight shillings a bottle would soon swamp a midshipman's monthly wine bill, which must not exceed fifteen to twenty shillings so some of us used to club together and get a bottle of the despised port.

Another day, when old " Twenty Stun " was in a much better state of mind, he told me some amusing stories about his Court experiences. Once at some function he stood on the Duke of Wellington's toes.

" You know, sir," he said, " I wasn't as 'eavy as I am now, but the Dook he turned round and d——d me for a hawkward fellow. Of course I couldn't 'elp it," he went on, " but His Grace was getting werry short-tempered—werry short-tempered."

Another day, after the usual question of " 'Ow are you getting on, sir ?" he began by saying, " Hexcuse me, sir, but are you any relation to —— —— ?"* mentioning a relative

* Field-Marshal Hugh, Viscount Gough, K.C.B.

of mine, who was a little bit of a celebrity in his way, and who had been doing a trifle of Empire-making at the head of a British army in India

I mentioned my relationship.

" Do you know, sir," said the old fellow, " hi attended 'im when he came to the castle to pay a wisit to the Queen. Oh, a fine old gentleman," he went on, " so straight and upright; quite the soldier, and werry liberal he was."

" Well, he ought to be; he has been a soldier since he was fifteen, and was at the taking of the Cape of Good Hope in 1795. He has got plenty of money, too, and ought to be able to give a good tip."

" So he did, sir—so he did. Do you know, sir," he went on, " you're werry like 'im."

" Am I ?"

" Yes," he said, " werry like 'im—just the same sort of look."

I never saw the likeness myself, although plenty of people used to tell me so, but it does not much matter now.

Another day old " Twenty Stun " began by

saying, " Hi wonder you didn't become a soldier, Mr. Gough."

" Why ?" I asked.

" Oh, a much better life, sir," he said. " No climbing up masts, and all that; lie in your bed all night, too."

" Well," I returned, " it's too late now; I am a sailor, you see."

" So I see, sir—so I see," he replied ; " but, all the same, it's a werry hard life, and you so young, sir. But you don't seem to mind it. Might I hask 'ow old you are ?"

" I am over fifteen," I said.

" Fifteen !" he said. " Why, you're little better than an hinfant. I wonder your mamma let you go."

" Why," I returned, " Prince Alfred is a midshipman, and he is as young as I am "

" Yes, sir," said old " Twenty Stun," with a twinkle in his eye, " but I expects he's a bit better looked after than you young gentlemen here. That dark gentleman, the Commander I think they calls him, seems werry sharp on you all."

" We have to learn our duty," said I.

" Just so, sir," replied he, " but it might be taught you a bit more kindly."

I expect that the old fellow had heard the Commander giving some of us a raking down. He was a kind-hearted old boy was " Twenty Stun," as I afterwards found out, but we must leave him and turn to the *Hero*.

On July 21 we ran into a heavy fog, a sure indication that we were approaching the banks of Newfoundland. We had to get up steam and go dead slow. The deep-sea lead-line was passed along, and we got a cast which gave us bottom at thirty fathoms. The fog continued during the night of the 21st and part of the 22nd, but in the afternoon it cleared away, and we proceeded full speed ahead. We were close in to the land, and expected to make it during the morning watch. A double set of lookouts was put on, as there were plenty of fishing-smacks about; we saw several of their lights, and heard their bells.

On the morning of the 23rd we sighted the high land about the entrance to St. John's

Harbour, and about ten o'clock we were close in. We did not proceed at once, as we wanted to give time for the Prince's reception. About twelve o'clock we went ahead again, and at two o'clock passed through the narrow entrance of the harbour. We anchored at 2.30 p.m., thirteen days out from Plymouth—a good passage for a heavy line-of-battle ship. Immediate preparations were made for the official landing of His Royal Highness.

H.M.S. *Styx* was lying in the harbour as the representative ship of the North American Squadron. The Governor, Sir Alexander Bannerman, sent his aide-de-camp off to inform us that everything was in readiness. In the interval the ship was surrounded by crowds of boats containing enthusiastic passengers, who frantically cheered the Prince whenever he made his appearance.

About four o'clock the State barge was manned, steered by a Lieutenant in full dress, assisted by a mate. Guard and band were drawn up, yards manned, and officers on deck in full dress. His Royal Highness made his appearance on the quarter-deck. He wore the full uniform of a Colonel in the British Army, with the ribbon and star of the Garter. It was the first time we had seen him in uniform, and everyone thought it became him admirably. He looked the Prince to perfection. The Duke of Newcastle wore the uniform of a Lord-Lieutenant—scarlet tail-coat with silver epaulettes. Lord St. Germans in Windsor dress, General Bruce and the equerries in the full uniform of their rank, completed the brilliant group that descended our gangway.

As the royal barge got about halfway to the shore, we fired a royal salute from our main-deck guns, and as His Royal Highness set foot for the first time on the shore of his future Canadian dominions, our lower-deck guns thundered out a second salute.

He was received by the Governor, and with all the pomp and state that the little community of fisherfolk could muster. The warmth and welcome of his reception might have been equalled, but it was never surpassed in any other part of the Empire.

The next day saw all hands on board the *Hero* hard at work refitting and cleaning the ship after our voyage. We took in about 200 tons of Cape Breton coal—filthy stuff it was, too; nearly drove the Commander demented. The first time we got up steam with it, it gave out dense columns of black smoke, which covered masts, yards, boats—in fact, anything it touched —with a thick coating of soot. The stuff stuck like grease, and no amount of soap, sand, and canvas could get it off. There was a big expenditure of Admiralty paint, which made the Halifax Dockyard authorities look aghast at our requisitions.

On shore all was gaiety. A levee was held by the Prince in the forenoon. Some of our officers went on shore to attend it; the rest of us, however, had to remain on board and look after our duties. We were to meet the Admiral at Halifax, and the Commander was determined to have the old ship in first-class order.

In the evening a grand ball was given, at which all our available officers were present. Of course it was full dress. A midshipman's

15

full dress always appears to me to be just the thing for a ball. It is not too stiff, like the uniforms of the higher ranks. In his blue tail coat lined with white satin, white waistcoat, and plain blue trousers, a dapper middy looks an ideal figure for a ballroom. I forget whether the ball was held in one of the public buildings or in one erected for the purpose. I think the latter, as none of the public buildings could have held the crowd present. All Newfoundland and its wives and daughters appeared to be present. The music was supplied by our band. The people declared that they had never heard anything like it. There was a popular gallop of the day called "The Night Bell," in which part of the band cease playing and sing the words. The effect on the Newfoundlanders was immense, and the gallop had to be repeated farther down the programme. All our officers were good dancing men; our Commander especially, although a short, stout man, was one of the best dancers I ever saw. He thought that dancing was part of a naval officer's duties. He had the midshipmen up to dance on the

main-deck when the band played at night, and
would sink his dignity and have a fly round with
one of us. If you could not dance, you had
your leave stopped until you learnt, so we were
all pretty proficient in the art.

The ball was opened by His Royal Highness
and the principal lady present. I think it was
the Governor's wife. After that, dancing became
general. The Prince danced with several other
ladies, and retired about twelve o'clock. Then
the fun became fast and furious. How I did
enjoy that ball! It was my first big one, and
it was something new to be made such a lot of.
The people could not show us enough attention.
One public functionary took the midshipmen
under his special care. There were any amount
of pretty girls present, and the public functionary found us plenty of partners. We were
all gone, however, on " a dark girl dressed in
blue," and went for the public functionary to
introduce us, which he did, and the pretty girl
had her card filled in no time.

We had a would-be swell in one of our marine
officers. She gave him a dance—more, I think,

for the sake of his red coat than anything else. After his turn was over, he came up to where the public functionary was plying a lot of us with champagne.

"Aw!" he said, sticking his eyeglass in his eye, and holding out his glass to be filled, "a sweetly pretty girl, and a very good dancer for a Colonial. Might I ask who she is?" he continued, as he finished his glass.

"Oh yes," said the public functionary vivaciously. "She is the daughter of our principal blacksmith!"

The Joey's jaw and eyeglass fell together.

"Aw!" repeated the discomfited amphibian warrior, as he turned on his heel amid a roar of laughter from those present. Anyway, never mind whether she was the daughter of blacksmith, whitesmith, or any other smith, she was a jolly nice girl, and danced like a fairy.

The ball broke up about four o'clock, and we made our way down to the boats. It was broad daylight, and none of us seemed very much the worse for wear. We had come through the first tussle without any casualties, with the exception of one of our surgeons. Some Newfoundlanders had collared his cocked hat; he in his turn had annexed an enormous bell-topper, which he had rammed down on his head. He sat in the stern-sheets of the boat, with his arms folded and a heavy scowl on his face; but whether the scowl was at the loss of his hat or too much New-foundland champagne we were too tired to be bothered about. At any rate, he presented a most laughable appearance with the bell-topper in conjunction with his epaulettes. Dog-tired as we were, we had to turn to at duty; but I often think of my first big ball at St. John's, and the pretty Newfoundland girl dressed in blue.

The Prince could not make a long stay at St. John's. He made a trip up the harbour on board H.M.S. *Styx*, and was shown all there was to be seen, being everywhere received with the utmost loyalty and enthusiasm. He won golden opinions on all sides by his appearance and gracious manner.

I got leave for the afternoon next day, and had a good look round. Three or four of us went a little way out of town, and as we were returning we were overtaken by His Royal Highness, who had been out riding. He was accompanied by the Governor and some of the suite. He pulled up, and in his usual kindly manner, asked us how we were enjoying ourselves. It was such little acts as this that made him so popular with us all.

On the 26th we were all ataunto again and ready for sea. The Prince embarked about 3 p.m. He was received on board with the usual royal honours. We immediately weighed and proceeded to sea, being escorted down the harbour by crowds of boats and small craft filled with loyal colonists, who were determined to see the last of His Royal Highness, who stood on the poop and acknowledged the farewell cheers with which he was greeted. We cleared the harbour about four o'clock, and shaped a course for Halifax, Nova Scotia, where we were due on July 30.

It was allowed by everyone that the Prince's visit to Newfoundland was a perfect success, and if His Royal Highness had been received with such demonstrations of loyalty by the small community, what would it be when we reached the larger centres of population later on?

There was one thing the Prince carried away with him in remembrance of Newfoundland—that was a present from the inhabitants of a magnificent Newfoundland dog. He was coal-black, of the purest breed, and about a year old. A circumstance occurred in connection with this dog which brought out the readiness with which the Prince grasped a situation. The dog had to have a name, and competition was invited from the suite and officers for a suitable one. A list of names was submitted to the Prince, but after a careful scrutiny none of them met with approval. It was with a smile that he handed back the list to the Commodore, who presented it.

"Perhaps Your Royal Highness would suggest a name yourself?" said the Commodore.

"Certainly," returned the Prince. "Call him Cabot."

It was a most happy thought, and a graceful little compliment to the memory of Sebastian Cabot, the discoverer of our oldest colony.

Cabot was put in charge of one of our first-class boys, and became a great pet on board. On our return he was sent up to Windsor Castle, accompanied by his keeper, and presented to the Queen and Prince Consort.

I believe that the Prince gained several prizes with him afterwards, and I have no doubt some of his descendants are in the possession of His Majesty, as such a noted lover and judge of dogs would be certain to keep the breed up.

CHAPTER VII

Arrival at Halifax, Nova Scotia—A great welcome—A week of gaiety—Lobster-spearing.

WE made a quiet passage down the coast of Cape Breton and Nova Scotia, and arrived off Halifax Harbour on the morning of our due date. I remember that morning well from a circumstance that took place. It was dead calm, and we were lying to, when suddenly a school of whales appeared all round us. The Prince and suite were interested in the gambols of the unwieldy monsters. I happened to be on the forecastle, and, boy-like, I was anxious to gain a nearer view of a novel sight, and got out on the bowsprit cap. From there I found my way down to the end of the dolphin-striker, and watched with eagerness for a whale to appear. My curiosity was more than satisfied. There was a sort of boil right underneath me, an enormous fellow showed his back above water,

121

there was a sound something between a snort and a snore, two columns of water ascended from his blow-holes, and the next instant I was as drenched as if I had fallen overboard. I lost no time in getting inboard, amid the broad grins of a number of bluejackets who had witnessed my discomfiture. I had enough of whale-seeing to suit me.

About twelve o'clock we steamed in towards the entrance of the harbour. The Prince was timed to land at two o'clock. Halifax is always associated by naval officers with pleasurable memories. The hospitality of the people, the good fishing, shooting, and other sport to be had, its bracing climate, which it needs a West Indian cruise to appreciate, all make it a favourite naval station.

Personally, I have more than a passing interest in Halifax. The lady who did me the honour to bear my name, and who has shared the ups and downs (mostly the downs, I am thinking) of my married life, is a Haligonian, so I always look back on Halifax with a double affection.

As we approached the harbour we could see headlands and points of vantage crowded; when we passed the wharves, more welcoming people were on them; and as we came in sight of the anchorage, a salute rang out from the citadel and men-of-war.

We steamed up past H.M.S. *Nile*, 91 guns, the flagship of Rear-Admiral Sir Alexander Milne, the Commander-in-Chief of the North American and West Indian station. The *Nile* presented a fine appearance, her manned yards, squared ports, taut rigging, well-stowed hammocks, all showed the well-ordered man-of-war. The other ships of the squadron were the *Cossack*, a 21-gun corvette, and the *Valorous*, 16 guns, a paddle-wheel frigate.

The *Hero* anchored off the dockyard. The Governor, the Earl of Mulgrave (afterwards the Marquis of Normanby), arrived on board to present his respects to the Prince. He was followed by the Admiral and General commanding the troops. After a short stay on board, the Governor and General left for the shore again, to be in readiness to receive the Prince. At two o'clock His Royal Highness left the *Hero* with the usual royal honours, and landed at the dock-yard.   He was received by the Governor and all the high functionaries of the colony.   Halifax could turn out a more imposing display than St. John's.   There were two regiments of the line in garrison—the 2nd Battalion of the 16th and the 1st Battalion of the 17th Regiments—now the same battalions of the Bedfordshire and Leicestershire Regiments.   The streets were lined with local Volunteers, the movement even in those days having extended to the Canadian colonies.   After a few addresses were presented, the Prince was driven to Government House, greeted by the cheers of the delighted and loyal inhabitants.

One of the addresses to His Royal Highness was presented in rather a strange manner, not without its touch of pathos.   The Mic-Mac Indians, the last remnant of a large tribe that once inhabited the shores of Halifax Harbour, had determined to present an address to the Prince.   They came down from their camp in a long line of birch-bark canoes gaily decorated,

GRAND CANOE RECEPTION GIVEN TO THE PRINCE OF WALES

To face page 24

but His Royal Highness had landed. After slowly paddling round the *Hero* two or three times, the poor Indians delivered the precious address to one of the boat-keepers of the boats lying astern. It was handed up, and duly forwarded on shore. The Prince immediately sent for the Indians, and spoke some kind and pleasant words to them, which filled them with delight. It was a touching incident, this meeting of the son and heir of the Great White Mother and the aboriginal inhabitants of the vast regions he would one day rule over. It was one of the kind and graceful acts on the part of the Prince such as endeared him to those brought in contact with him. He was quick to think of what would please and gratify.

For a week Halifax gave itself up to a regular round of gaiety. When the Haligonians start to do a thing they do it well—levees, balls, dinners, sport, all were provided for the Prince and his suite; unbounded hospitality was shown to the officers and men of the Royal Canadian Squadron. The Commander was liberal in his leave, and the junior officers of the ships got their fair share of all that was going.

A splendid military ball was given by the officers of the garrison, at which I was present. I was lucky in having one of our county neighbours a Captain in the 17th Regiment. As soon as he could he was off to see me, and was almost wild with delight at the meeting. We had been cronies at home, and our people were friends. He had been out over three years, and was eager to know all the county news.

He was a very young Captain. His people being wealthy, he had purchased all his steps. He promised all sorts of sport, amongst others a moose-hunt. Our time at Halifax was limited to a week, so the moose-hunt did not come off. But when the *Hero* came out again on the station at a subsequent part of her commission, I had the pleasure of shooting a moose under my friend's auspices. To my readers I may explain that the moose is another name for the elk. Moose steak was a common dish in Halifax hotels and restaurants, and very good it tasted.

The garrison ball at Halifax in honour of

the Prince was a splendid success. Soldiers certainly know how to do the thing well, and this time they excelled. On each side of the Prince's daïs the colours of the two regiments were grouped, attended by their escort. The decorations were superb, and displayed great taste in their arrangement. The music was supplied by the bands of the 16th and 17th Regiments, stationed in outside galleries on each side of the ballroom, screened off by masses of flowering shrubs. A curious effect, and one I have never heard since in a ballroom, was the music of the quadrilles played in alternate sets by the bands, the final by the combined bands. It was very good.

My friend was one of the stewards, and looked after me most attentively. I was quite proud of him. He was a very handsome fellow, with very fair hair and a long golden moustache. As he flitted about among the guests in his scarlet coat, well groomed and well set up, I thought he was a credit to the old county at home. After supper he told me he was going to introduce me to his fiancée, and presently he led me up to a very pretty girl. As he mentioned my name, he coupled it with the remark, "One of my county neighbours." I expect the rogue had an object in view.

His people were a very exclusive old family. He knew that I would be home before him, and that I would be sure to be asked about the young lady's appearance. I certainly was a willing herald as I fell a slave at once to the fair Haligonian's bright eyes, and when I did get home sang her praises to such an extent that my mother remarked, "I expect you will marry a Halifax girl yourself some day, Tom" Little did she think what a prophetess she was. However, when the young lady did arrive at home as the wife of my friend, she quite held her own in a county famed for the beauty of its women.

Our stay at Halifax was rapidly drawing to a close. His Royal Highness was going overland to New Brunswick and on to Prince Edward's Island. We were to pick him up at Charlottetown. Before we sailed we were initiated into the mysteries of lobster-spearing.

It was most exciting sport. A moonlight night was chosen. It was necessary to procure pine-wood torches from the Mic-Mac settlement. Most of us provided ourselves with a spear, but they could be hired on shore. The weapon is only a spear in name, it is a light pole with a flexible fork at the end. After dark we got one of the ship's boats, the third cutter, or jolly-boat, with about two of the boat's crew, pulled to the shore, lay in the oars, and kept in about four or five feet of water. A torch was lit and stuck in the bows of the boat, whilst the men poled her along with the boat-hooks; the spearers stood on the thwarts. In a minute or two lobsters could be seen crawling along the bottom from all directions, attracted by the light. As soon as a big fellow was near enough, down went the spear until the spearer got it right over the lobster, when by a well-directed prod he drove the flexible fork over his back, gave a twist of the hand, and brought the fellow up, claws waving and tail snapping, and shook him off into the bottom of the boat.

Really, the fun was glorious. As a rule, the

17

first shots were missed, until the spearers became accustomed to the depth and deceptive look of the water; but as we got our hands in we would bring up a lobster every time. Half a dozen midshipmen lobster-spearing is a subject for laughter. Of course the best places are in the bows of the boat; the light shed from the torch is stronger. Those aft have a poorer chance, but places are changed so as to give everyone a show. As the excitement increased, the spearers got careless about how they shook their catches off spears, and some of us got a clawing lobster landed on shoulders, where it took hold. On such occasions the language was lurid. As for the bottom of the boat, he would be a venturesome mid who would step off the thwarts, for he would be the object of attack from a clawing, fighting mass of lobsters, not at all averse to making common cause against one of their captors. The night wound up by landing at some sheltered cove, where a roaring fire was built among the fir-trees. The refreshments were produced. Some of the catch were barbecued—that is, a hole was made in the red-hot ashes, and a live lobster dropped in and covered up.

I don't suppose the process is any more cruel than dropping a live lobster into a pot of boiling water, although it sounds worse. Barbecued lobster is a toothsome morsel to a party of hungry fishers.

Our stay at Halifax wound up with a grand picnic given by the residents up Bedford Basin. Halifax Harbour expands a few miles above the town into a magnificent sheet of water, perfectly landlocked with good holding ground. It is in the form of a complete circle, and capable of holding the whole British Navy, with plenty of room to spare. Bedford Basin is, I should think, the finest natural harbour on the east coast of North America, and the British Empire is the happy possessor of it.

The Prince having ended his visit to Halifax and started inland to visit New Brunswick, we got ready for sea. The squadron weighed and proceeded under steam for Charlottetown. Our route lay north-east up the coast of Nova Scotia, and through the Gut of Canso, a picturesque strait separating Nova Scotia from Cape Breton.

We had as passengers the Countess of Mulgrave and Lady Laura Phipps. They occupied the Prince's quarters for the time being. The passage was made leisurely, as we had plenty of time, the *Hero* arriving at Charlottetown about August 7.

The residents of the quiet though prosperous island vied in their readiness to show hospitality to us. We were crowded all day with anxious sightseers. The visit of a British squadron was not an everyday occurrence at Charlottetown, as we were made well aware of.

The Prince arrived about a couple of days after we anchored, and was received with great demonstrations of loyalty. - The Prince Edward Islanders have always been credited with intense devotion to the Crown, and they sustained the reputation with all the power at their command. His Royal Highness could only spare a day or two to the loyal islanders. He had a long tour before him through Canada and the United States, but the short stay was devoted to hos-

pitality and gaiety, of which we came in for a big share.

On August 10 we received the Prince and suite on board again. It was getting quite dark at the time, and the last glimpse I had of Charlottetown was the houses illuminated by the flashes of our lower-deck guns as they thundered out a royal salute as welcome to His Royal Highness. Everyone seemed pleased to have him on board again. Shortly afterwards we weighed and proceeded on our voyage to Quebec. We were going to make the passage under steam, as we were now in narrow seas. We had a St. Lawrence pilot on board, but he proved himself of little account, as subsequent events showed.

The *Hero* was to call at Gaspe Bay, situate at the southern entrance to the St. Lawrence, where the Prince was to land for a few hours. We reached there on the morning of the 12th, and anchored about a mile out. The royal barge was hoisted out, and His Royal Highness and some of the suite landed. Guns were taken, and some shooting was looked for. I believe

18

the place then abounded with game. The royal party got a little sport, and after being on shore for some time, returned to the ship. It was a purely private visit, as the locality was sparsely populated. The *Hero* remained at anchor all night, and got under way early next morning. We shaped a course across the St. Lawrence for the Saguenay River, the scenery of which is very grand, and the Governor-General and the Canadian Government were to meet and welcome the Prince there. We were under easy steam all that day, and next morning, August 14, we arrived off the mouth of the river. An unfortunate thing happened here.

The St. Lawrence pilot, who professed a complete knowledge of the locality, had charge of the ship, and we steamed slowly in, every precaution being taken. Experienced leadsmen were in the chains, when suddenly there was a slight shock and grating sound, and the *Hero* was hard and fast on shore.

We were at breakfast in the gun-room at the time. The ship heeled over to a dangerous degree, but the lower-deck ports were promptly lowered and barred in, so we had to light the gun-room lamps. On taking soundings, we found the ship was hanging on a pinnacle-rock, just before the foremast, with deep water all round. There was a rising tide. We waited for about half an hour, and then went full speed astern, and the old ship came off the rock. We rubbed off about ten feet of our false keel, which floated up alongside. However, we were making no water. We anchored about a couple of cables' length from the scene of our disaster.

A steamer had come down from Quebec, bringing the Governor-General, Sir Edmond Head, and some members of the Canadian Ministry. They came on board to welcome the Prince. Preparations were made for the trip up the Saguenay. The *Flying Fish*, our despatch gunboat, was going to take the royal and viceregal party up.

Owing to the delay attendant on the ship going ashore, a start could not be made that day. The Governor-General and Ministry were entertained at dinner by His Royal Highness, and returned to their quarters on board their steamer.

Next morning an early start was made. His Royal Highness and suite, the viceregal party, and some of our officers went on board the *Flying Fish*. She shortly afterwards weighed, and in a few minutes disappeared through the cleft in the wall of rock that forms the entrance to the river. The scenery is stupendously grand, and the royal party was much impressed by it. The *Flying Fish* fired her heavy bow gun to show the effect of the echoes among the overhanging walls of rock.

The Prince's party returned about dusk. The Governor-General and Ministers went on board their steamer, and proceeded to Quebec to be in readiness to receive His Royal Highness. We remained at anchor that night, as we were not due at Quebec until the 18th.

CHAPTER VIII

Quebec—Hospitality of the Canadians—The reception at
Toronto—The Orangeman's arch—Off to Niagara.

On the morning of the 17th of August the *Hero*
weighed anchor, and we proceeded up the
St. Lawrence under steam, followed by our consorts, the *Ariadne* and *Flying Fish*. The river
banks were just visible, and we were impressed
by the width of the magnificent stream. We
made steady progress all day, but in the afternoon the ebb-tide checked our way to such an
extent that, although we were under full steam,
the ship was not doing much more than six
knots. The *Hero* anchored for the night at
such a distance below Quebec as would enable
us to land the Prince at our allotted time—
4 p.m.—on the 18th. We got under way again
early on that day. As we steamed up and
began to approach Quebec, smoke on the horizon
ahead indicated that we were to be met and

137

welcomed afloat by the loyal Canadians. Early
in the forenoon we could make out a fleet of
river steamers bearing down on us. As the Royal
Squadron came up, the steamers stopped, headed
upstream, and formed two lines, through which
we passed. They were the pick of the St. Lawrence steamers, and appeared strange to us with
their great paddle-boxes, towering deck-houses,
and walking-beams. ˙ They were all crammed
with enthusiastic Canadians, and decorated with
bunting, displaying all manner of loyal welcomes. Two of the largest took their stations
on the *Hero's* quarters, and steadily kept their
places until we anchored.

One of them, the *Passport*, attracted our
attention by her fine appearance and the ease
with which she kept up with us. The crowds
on board cheered His Royal Highness to the
echo whenever he made his appearance. He
bowed his acknowledgments, only to be greeted
by more cheers and frantic waving of pocket-
handkerchiefs. As we came nearer, the flotilla
was increased by smaller steamers and sailing
craft, all crowded.

To add éclat to the scene, the band was got up on the poop, and we treated the fair Canadians on board the steamers to all the latest quadrilles and valses. Much amusement was caused by the people on board one of the craft, who promptly got up a quadrille-party, and danced away to the notes of our powerful band floating across the water. The Quebecers, with their strain of French blood, could not let good dance-music go to waste. The officers on the poop watched the dancers through their telescopes. I never heard the same set of quadrilles played afterwards but it brought the scene to my recollection.

About two o'clock we were in sight of Quebec, and could make out Citadel Point. A fine view was obtained of the Falls of Montmorency, with their fall of 230 feet. The *Hero* arrived at the end of her voyage about three o'clock, and anchored off Quebec amid the thunder of guns, the strains of music, and the welcoming cheers of the loyal inhabitants.

At 3.45 His Royal Highness left the *Hero* for the shore with the usual royal honours. He took leave of the assembled officers who were grouped on the quarter-deck, shaking hands with the Commodore and Commander, and bowing to the others. As the silken standard came fluttering down from our main-topgallant masthead, we felt that we had done our duty well in conveying His Royal Highness across the Atlantic without a hitch, and without even letting a drop of sea-spray touch him. Her Majesty the Queen and H.R.H. the Prince Consort had full confidence in committing the safe-keeping of the heir-apparent to the British Navy.

The Prince on landing was received by the Governor-General and Canadian Ministry, and by no section of the people was he more welcomed than by the French-Canadians, who are French in name, language, and religion, but British in their loyalty and devotion to the Crown.

It was a masterpiece of statesmanship, the visit of the Prince of Wales to Canada. The nation had recently passed through the fiery ordeal of the Indian Mutiny. The Canadians

THE PRINCE OF WALES LANDING AT QUEBE

were neighbours of a great English-speaking republic, prosperous beyond measure, and with no sign of the terrible rent that actually took place the following year. There was undoubtedly a feeling between certain sections of the American people and English-Canadians that it would be for the welfare of the latter if they were absorbed into the great republic. The wave of loyalty that passed over Canada on the occasion of the Prince's visit drowned most of that feeling, and the break-up of the American Republic the next year killed anything that was left of it.

The Royal Squadron was to remain in Quebec for some time, as the Prince's tour through Canada and the United States would occupy about two months. The officers were treated with the usual hospitality of the Canadians, and attended all the gaieties consequent on His Royal Highness's visit. But the Canadian Government were determined to show the officers something more than balls, picnics, and the like. They wanted them to see their wonderful inland lakes, or rather seas, and to visit that wonder of the world, the Falls of Niagara. Every officer was to receive a free pass over the Canadian Trunk Railway, free steamboat passages, free hotel accommodation, and free drinks if desired, with cigars thrown in. That was doing the thing properly. When it was first announced in the gun-room at breakfast one morning, the excitement was immense. One half the officers were to go on leave at once, and the remainder when they returned. The trip would take about three weeks, and parties were made up to travel together. My party was to go on the second leave, and we saw our messmates start off full of the hope of a rattling good time.

The routine of the ship was carried on by the remaining officers, the First-Lieutenant being executive officer, as the Commander had gone up with the first batch; he was liberal in giving leave to the youngsters, and I had a good share of it. My first day on shore at Quebec was one to be remembered by me, ending up with a laughable incident, occasioned by a midshipman professing to be a first-class linguist. His knowledge of the French language proved to be an expensive luxury, as it turned out.

A party of us went on shore on a day's leave. After ordering dinner at an hotel, we sallied out to see the sights. We were anxious to see the Heights of Abraham· and Wolfe's Monument. As it is some little distance from the city, we agreed to hire a fiacre, and left the gentleman who said he could speak French to engage the cabby. He returned in a few minutes and informed us it was all right. He led us to a slap-up turnout. Before we got in he said that he had arranged with the driver to take us all round the `sights for two dollars—in gold, he added. Why gold? we all wondered; perhaps the cabby thought we did not understand the currency. As the jovial crew boarded the vehicle, our friend aired his French again to the driver who stood, hat in hand, bowing and smiling.

" Oui, oui, certainement," he replied.

" What's wrong?" asked one of our fellows.

" Oh, nothing," was the answer. "I was only repeating the terms; it's all right, two dollars. In gold," he added.

" He's devilish particular about his gold," said another mid. " However, I suppose it's all right."

" Now, then, gee up, coachy!" he called out. " Oui, oui, avancer, cocher," repeated our French scholar, with a sort of " What do you think of *that*, you fellows ?" air.

The *cocher* cracked his whip, and away we went. We drove out to the scene of the historic battle, and saw where Wolfe fell, had a turn round into the country, lunched at a wayside hotel, and got back to Quebec about half an hour before our dinner-hour. As we arrived we began to talk about settling; the bother was about the two dollars in gold. After a long discussion, it was finally agreed to give the driver half a sovereign, that being more than the fare that we understood had been arranged for. As we alighted from the fiacre we deputed the engagee to settle with the driver. On tendering the half-sovereign he was met with " Non, non," and a torrent of Canadian-French which quite took the wind out of our friend's sails. We looked to him for an explanation.

"The beggar certainly said 'deux dollars d'or,'" he answered.

"Non, non," said the cabby; "deux dollars d'heure."

His strong patois in pronouncing *d'heure* had evidently misled our friend to mistake the word for *d'or*. There was the making of a nice little scene in the street; a party of British midshipmen were not going to allow themselves to be sat upon by a French-Canadian cabby. Any further trouble was stopped by the lucky arrival of a Quebec gentleman whom some of us knew. We appealed to him, and in a few minutes he heard both sides of the story. Telling the driver to wait, we went into the hotel together. Our friend pointed out that the cabman was only asking his legal fare, two dollars an hour. We had been out about six hours—twelve dollars in all (about £2 10s.); it was an expensive outing for us, especially as we had ordered dinner, which would have to be paid for. The Quebec gentleman said he would endeavour to arrange with the cabman. After a long parley, accompanied by much shrugging of shoulders and holding out of hands, M. Cocher agreed to accept £1 10s., which we gladly paid. After declining our invitation to dinner then, but accepting one on board the *Hero* at a later date, our friend left us.

We sat down, rather apprehensive of our ability to square up for the dinner. The charge, however, turned out to be very moderate. After discharging it, we had enough to pay for our boat off to the ship, and returned, a sadder and wiser party of midshipmen, with the firm resolution never to trust to the services of the French scholar again, who was unmercifully chaffed about his French, which he said he had learned in Jersey when he was at school.

A few days after our adventure, some of the first batch of officers returned from their leave, full of glowing accounts of the good time they had had. It was arranged that the second lot of officers should start on the following Monday. As I was to be one of them, I was full of excitement at the prospect.

The few days before we started on our trip up the St. Lawrence were taken up in arranging the details of our journey. There was one advantage in being in the second party, as we benefited by the experiences of the first. The time at our disposal was limited, and we wanted to make the most of it. Six of us agreed to form one party. We were all of the same standing in the service, had been in the training-ship together, and four of us were school-fellows at Dr. Burney's celebrated naval academy, whose boys were generally known throughout the service as " Burney's Bull-dogs." Our Second-Lieutenant was going up with us, and we unanimously agreed to make him leader and treasurer. We contributed £10 each to the common fund; not that much money would be required, as all our expenses were borne by the Canadian Government, but it was as well to be on the safe side. The free passes we received were neat folding-tickets of blue morocco, with the Prince's feathers on the front cover and the Canadian arms on the back. On opening the ticket, on one side was printed a list of the leading towns; opposite to them were the names of one or two principal hotels.

We had only to present our tickets at the hotel door, when our party was immediately bowed into the best accommodation the house afforded. Our route was by rail to Montreal and Toronto, across Lake Ontario, and return by steamer.

It was a beautiful September morning when we pulled on shore to catch the early train from Quebec to Montreal. The train started from the south side of the river opposite the town, the line running on that side until Montreal was reached, but I presume there is railway communication on both sides now. We were amused at the American style of carriage, which none of us had ever seen before, but as we took our seats and got our traps stowed away, we found them very comfortable. After we started, we found our way out on the end-platforms, and, boy-like, we took a delight in the novelty. At all the stations we had plenty of time to get out and stretch our legs. We attracted a good deal of attention, as it had been arranged that two of us were to appear in uniform each day during our journey, so as to give a distinctive character to our party. The simple country folk stared

at those in uniform. I suppose it was the first time that a British midshipman had been seen in his war-paint in those regions.

We reached Montreal at evening, and crossed the new Victoria Bridge, the last rivet of which had been driven by the Prince only a few days before. We had not much opportunity of seeing its noble proportions, as it was dark; but on our return journey we were shown over the bridge by the general manager of the Canadian Grand Trunk Railway. We drove to the St. Lawrence Hall, one of the hotels mentioned on our tickets, and on our Lieutenant presenting his, we were received with great *empressement*, and shown to a private drawing-room, where we were presently interviewed by the bowing proprietor, who expressed his regret that we were late for dinner, "but if he had been aware we were coming, he would have had it kept for us." He went on to say that, "in a few minutes, he would have a table laid in a private dining-room and something got ready. In the meantime he had ordered a bitter." He rang the bell, and a waiter made his appearance with champagne cocktails, a drink much in vogue during the Prince's visit. After the cocktails and a wash, we sat down to a fine supper, with all sorts of Canadian and American delicacies, to which our hungry crew did full justice. We had a stroll round before turning in, but as it was pretty late, and we were dog-tired with the train journey, we did not see much.

Next morning, after breakfast, we did the streets and Notre Dame Cathedral, but as we intended to stay over on our return journey, we reserved the sights until then.

The journey was resumed that evening. Our party had our first experience of sleeping-cars. They were certainly not Pullman-cars. After a night in them we came to the conclusion that a hammock was much more comfortable. Two of our mids scandalized a sour-faced Presbyterian minister by a terrific bolster-fight in the gangway, and had to be called to order by our Lieutenant, who was awakened by the row.

We reached Toronto about four o'clock next forenoon. We repeated our experiences of Montreal, and found rooms at a leading hotel,

being treated with every courtesy. Toronto
was very full. The Prince was expected to
arrive next day, and arches and decorations
were going up in all directions. There was a
bitter sectarian feeling existing in Toronto
between the Orangemen and the Catholics. The
Orangemen had erected a fine arch with repre-
sentations of King William III. on his horse
crossing the Boyne, and the usual mottoes
about "the glorious, pious, immortal memory,"
etc., all draped with orange and blue.

The Duke of Newcastle heard about this
arch, and sent word that the Prince would not
drive under it. As the arch occupied one of
the best sites in a principal thoroughfare, this
was rather awkward. After a lot of persuasion,
the Orangemen consented to remove the ob-
noxious emblems, which they did muttering
threats at the Duke's unfairness. The Duke,
however, was perfectly right : so far no sectarian
feeling had been allowed to mar the Prince's
visit, all religious bodies having been treated
alike. The Duke was a master of tact, but the
Orangemen proved too much for him after all.

The mounted king was taken down, and the arch covered with loyal mottoes and devices. On the occasion of the Prince's entry into Toronto he drove under the redecorated arch; when he left the city he drove under it again. As he cleared it there was a sound of falling boards, a cheer from the Orangemen, and on the Duke looking back, the Orange emblems and mottoes appeared in all their glory: the others had only been dummies, and His Royal Highness had driven under both. I don't think it was a nice trick to play, and the leading papers commented adversely on the bad taste displayed by the Orangemen of Toronto.

The Prince arrived from Ottawa the next day, and the Toronto people gave him a great reception. We had capital-places provided for us (of course, we appeared in uniform), and as we looked upon His Royal Highness as being under our special charge, although he was ashore, we cheered and waved our caps to such an extent that we attracted the notice of Major Teesdale, who pointed us out to the Prince. His Royal Highness bowed and smiled to his

THE PRINCE OF WALES IN CANADA: THE ORANGEMEN'S ARCH
AT TORONTO

To face page 152

faithful midshipmen's salute. We felt quite proud to see him looking so well, and at the loyal greeting he was getting.

There was a great ball at Toronto that evening, which we attended. Our Lieutenant, after the reception was over, called on Major Teesdale, who informed him that the Prince wished the *Hero's* officers present in Toronto to attach themselves to his suite that night. The ball was a grand affair, and we had plenty of dancing. The six midshipmen attending His Royal Highness came in for a great deal of curious notice; people thought that we were pages; but when they learnt that we were middies of the ship that brought His Royal Highness across the Atlantic, the notice became even more marked. We were very proud boys for a day or two afterwards, and stood a good chance of being spoilt.

We left Toronto on the afternoon of the same day as the Prince, and took passage across Lake Ontario for Niagara. Our steamer was a fine specimen of the American lake or river boat; I forget her name. The accommodation on board was most sumptuous, and when we sat down to dinner in her superb saloon, with its glittering lights, fine table appointments, and host of black waiters, we thought of the *Hero's* gun-room in a gale of wind—the ports barred in, we holding on to our plates to prevent them fetching away across the table, and the atmosphere enough to poison a horse.

We had a good look all round the steamer, from her boilers and furnaces on the lower-deck to the great walking-beam on the top of all. It was all a source of curiosity to deep-sea sailors. After dinner we went on to the hurricane-deck. It was a bright moonlight night, and we were out of sight of land, yet we were on fresh water. The lake was quite calm, but we were told by the Captain that a nasty short sea gets up when there is any wind.

Next morning we were steaming up the mouth of the Niagara River, and stopped at Queens-town. We had to cross the river to the American side to get the train for Niagara Falls. We here experienced our first sample of the United States. Being an American line, our passes were not available, and we had to pay the fare.

THE PRINCE OF WALES IN CANADA: HIS ROYAL HIGHNESS DESCENDING A TIMBER-SLIDE
AT OTTAWA

Our Lieutenant wanted tickets for us. As we had no American money, he tendered English gold; but the impudent booking-clerk looked at it and returned it, saying he "reckoned the British Queen's head on metal was no good this side." Luckily, it was some time before the train started, and one of us went over the river again and interviewed the purser of the steamer, who changed some of our money, the messenger coming back again with a roll of filthy dollar-notes, with which we satisfied the exacting clerk. Shortly afterwards we started, and had a pleasant run up the American side of the river. I must say we found the American train much superior to the Canadian Grand Trunk. A boy with books came through the carriages with all the latest novels at American prices. I bought Wilkie Collins's "Woman in White" for $12\frac{1}{2}$ cents. In Canada it was 6s.

We crossed over the splendid railway suspension bridge into Canadian territory again. As we did so, we obtained a fine view of the Falls; it was our first glimpse of them, and we were all excited at the sight. It was a curious thing to us to be asked by the Customs officer " if we had anything to declare." As if we had had any chance to pick up any dutiable articles during our short trip on American soil! I forgot my book, however, and might have had it collared if the Customs man had seen it. We drove to Clifton House—a fine hotel right opposite the Falls. On presenting our passes, we were shown the greatest civility by the manager. A fine sitting-room, looking out on the river, was allotted to us, and three special niggers.

CHAPTER IX

Niagara—Wreck of the *Lady Elgin*—Mr. Herbert Ingram, proprietor of the *Illustrated London News*, and his son amongst the victims—Blondin—The peach orchard.

NIAGARA has been so often described by many able pens, and the photographer has brought the wonderful scene so home to all parts of the world, that to attempt further description of it is only to repeat what many of us are familiar with. My first impression of the Falls, I remember, have been shared by many who have been privileged to look on the glorious sight, and that is a sense of disappointment. One has the imagination worked up to such a pitch that the real thing at first sight falls short of what fancy painted it. But after a day's sight-seeing fancy disappears in the Cave of the Winds, or takes a header from the top of the Terrapin Tower (now demolished), and fascination takes its place; you return again and again to the same spot, until you are reminded that there are other views to be visited, and fresh vistas of splendour present themselves to you.

The Clifton House, our hotel, was charmingly situated, within a few hundred yards of the Falls. After a sumptuous breakfast, at which our party of midshipmen astonished the natives by the amount of good things they stowed away, we sallied forth to do the Falls. Our first visit was to Table Rock, a platform of rock just on the lip of the Canadian Fall. After a good view there, we went up to the Rapids, and then down to the foot of the Falls. In the afternoon we crossed the ferry just below them to the American side. Singular to say, the surface water for some distance below the Falls is quite calm; but it has a deadly oily look that is even worse than turmoil, and evidently hides a tremendous current underneath. We visited Goat Island and the Terrapin Tower; this last always struck me as being a point where the view was most sublime. It was a stone tower, built on a rock situated right on the brink of the Horse-

shoe or Canadian Fall, and connected with Goat
Island by a light iron bridge. How on earth
they first reached the point puzzled me, unless
they flew over. The rush of water between
Goat Island and the tower was terrific. Once
on top, you looked down right into the centre
of the Canadian Fall, and you were impressed
with the grandeur of the scene. The depth of
water poured over the lip of the precipice was
indicated by its deep green colour. We were
told that it must have been over twenty feet
deep, which was proved by sending a vessel
drawing that depth of water over the fall and
her not touching bottom—rather an expensive
way of taking soundings, I am thinking.

We then visited the Cave of the Winds, walking right under the Falls. Before returning to
our hotel we had a trip in the *Maid of the Mist*.
This was a miniature American river steamer,
which used to steam right up to the face of the
Falls, and almost shove her nose into the water.
As it was, you had to don a suit of oilskins for
the short but venturesome voyage, otherwise
you would have been wet to the skin. The fare

was half a dollar, oilskins thrown in, and it was certainly cheap at the money. The *Maid of the Mist* was the property of a man called Joel Robinson. He had built his little craft on the spot. In the year following our visit the venture proved unprofitable, and Robinson was offered a good price for his steamer, but had to deliver her at the mouth of the Niagara River. This involved him running through the whirlpool, where Captain Webb was subsequently drowned.

The daring trip was resolved upon, the crew of the little boat being Robinson, the engineer, another dare-devil, and a third man as deck-hand. The banks of the river were crowded with people to witness the voyage. The steamer started, and she got on all right until she was well into the Rapids. On approaching the whirl-pool a full head of steam was kept on, but she was thrown on her beam ends, the smoke-stack carried away, whilst the people on the banks held their breath, expecting her to be smashed up; but the gallant little craft came through all right, and Robinson got his money. On re-turning to the hotel, we found everyone in a state of excitement. News of a terrible catastrophe had just arrived. The *Lady Elgin* steamer had sailed from Chicago full of passengers on September 7, and came into collision with a schooner. The steamer shortly afterwards sank, and nearly everyone on board perished. Amongst those who were lost was Mr. Herbert Ingram and his eldest son. Mr. Ingram was the founder and sole proprietor of the *Illustrated London News*. He had only left Clifton House a few days before our arrival, and universal sorrow was expressed at his untimely death.

The *Illustrated London News* was at that time the only medium of bringing before the public the events of the day depicted by leading artists. The paper was represented on the Prince of Wales's tour by Mr. G. H. Andrews, R.W.S., as special correspondent and artist. His spirited sketches brought before the British public the doings of the heir-apparent during his absence from England, whilst his written description of the same was the most reliable in any British paper.

We met a gentleman at Niagara who was shortly afterwards designed to play an important part in the struggle that broke out in the United States the following year. This was Colonel MacGruder, of the United States Army. His object in visiting Niagara was to invite the Prince to visit the frontier post which he commanded, to indulge in some buffalo-hunting. The Colonel used to charm us by his stories of wild adventure with the Indians and hunters. It was like Fenimore Cooper's novels. He was a man of splendid presence, bronzed from his prairie life, with a great sweeping brown moustache and glittering eagle eyes—a veritable leader of men. As for his manners, I never saw them surpassed.

Midshipmen are generally good judges of what constitutes a gentleman. They are invariably boys of good family, and they are keen to detect any bad form in a man. I can look back on a long experience of men, from a king to a pirate, and I can say that I never met a more high-bred gentleman than this gallant American. He was a Southerner, and when the War of Secession broke out, he threw in his lot with his native State (I think he was a Virginian), and received a high command in the Southern Army. He became a celebrated cavalry leader, and as such was the equal of General J. B. Stewart in his daring raids and dashing surprises on the enemy. As the war progressed, I was always on the lookout for the exploits of General MacGruder, of the Confederate States Army.

I may say that the Colonel had an interview with the Prince, but His Royal Highness was unable to accept his invitation, as his time was all allotted. He had, however, a couple of days prairie-hen shooting under the Colonel's auspices, as the picture testifies. That buffaloes were plentiful enough in those days was evidenced by a story the Colonel told us. A short time before, the whole of the horses of his command had been stampeded by a countless herd of buffaloes, which rushed through his camp, the tents and equipages being trodden to bits, his men only escaping the same fate by rushing to a small hill which divided the herd. He described it as a living sea of shaggy heads and horns.

We had a celebrity at Niagara during our visit. This was Blondin, who was going to walk across the river just below the suspension bridge. Numbers of visitors came to view the sight. We went down on the morning of the day to have a look at the rope. It was a white Manila one, two inches in diameter, and drawn as taut as it could be; it was further steadied by numerous guys on each side. The performance was to take place at 3 p.m. Before that time both banks of the river and the bridge were crowded with people. We got a capital place close to the rope. Punctual to time, Blondin made his appearance, arrayed in the usual acrobatic costume, and carrying a long balancing-pole. Bowing to acknowledge the cheers he was greeted with, he stepped on to the rope as cool as if it was a street pavement, and walked out into the middle of the chasm, bowed again to the breath - bound spectators, and finished his walk to the American side in a leisurely style. In a few minutes he repeated the performance, and re-crossed.

The second part was carrying a man across on his back. When he made his appearance with the man perched upon his shoulders, he looked all right, but the man was very pale. Blondin advanced this time with more caution, carefully picking his steps. In the middle a halt took place, and it was evident some hitch had occurred, but Blondin soon resumed his perilous journey amid great cheering.

We afterwards learnt that the man lost his nerve, and Blondin threatened to put him down in the middle and let him shift for himself. If he had fallen with his burden, they would have fallen into water, but whether they would have come up again is another matter.

Blondin repeated his performance before the Prince a few days afterwards. He also wheeled a barrow over, and offered to wheel His Royal Highness over to American territory; but the Canadian authorities decided that the Prince would make his entrance into the United States in a little more dignified style.

22

To show the state of feeling in Canada against Sir E. Head, the Governor-General, one paper, commenting on the above offer, said that "it was out of the question allowing our beloved Prince to incur the dangers of such a journey, but if it was the Governor-General, the thanks of the community should be given to Blondin if he wheeled Sir Edmond to American soil, never to return." The paper then went on to say that "the satisfaction would be increased if the wheeler was Old Nick himself wheeling the Governor - General to Hades amid the usual sulphurous smoke and flames." I don't think any Australian paper has ever gone as far as that against any un-popular Governor. I don't remember what the unfortunate Sir Edmond had done, but the fact remained that he was highly disliked by a certain section of the Canadians.

Our stay at Niagara was drawing to a close. Every day we were sight-seeing; always finding fresh beauties, and becoming more and more enchanted with the Falls. I have often met people who have expressed the same idea : they have gone there with the intention of remaining two or three days, and have extended their visit to a month.

Our leave was nearly up, and we had to be on board the *Hero* in little over a week. Before we left, a gentleman staying at Clifton House invited us to visit a peach orchard he owned, not far from Queenstown, on the Niagara River. It was a beautiful Canadian autumn day—the "fall," as it is termed—when we started on our trip, and the trees were beginning to assume the gorgeous tints that they do in Canada at that period of the year. Our friend said it was the beginning of the Indian summer. He had provided conveyances for us, and we reached the peach orchard after a beautiful drive. We were taken by surprise at the size of it and the luxuriance of the fruit. The branches of the trees were breaking down under the weight, and in many instances had to be propped up.

To English boys, who only know the peach as a wall-fruit, the sight was novel. Our entertainer did not let us look very long.

"Now, boys," said he, "pitch in, and when

you think you can't eat any more, come up to the farm-house and have some peach brandy, and you will be able to attack them again."

Pitch in we did.

I don't think any peach orchard in North America had such an onslaught made on it before. How we revelled in the luscious fruit! One fellow started to keep count of the peaches he put away: he got up to nine dozen, and then gave it up. We were beginning to slacken off, when the owner came down with a bottle of peach brandy, a boy following with a can of water and glasses. We had a nip all round · rare stuff it was, too, and had a wonderful effect in stimulating an appetite for another attack on the fruit. At last we got careless about them, and took to pelting each other. I remember planting a big overripe peach right in the back of the neck of one of our party. At the same time a fellow filled my ear and collar by a well-directed shot of a more than overripe one.

At last a bell rang at the farm-house, and we heard our friend singing out to us to come up to lunch. He had a glorious spread of fish,

HIS ROYAL HIGHNESS THE PRINCE OF WALES SHOOTING ON THE PRAIRIES OF THE FAR WEST

To face page 168

flesh, and fowl, with buckwheat cakes, maple sugar, and other Canadian delicacies. After lunch, two of us were furnished with guns, and went out for a shot. There were plenty of pigeons about. My companion was my top-mate, T., and we were accompanied by a farm-hand with a dog. We shot several pigeons, and were going through some long grass when I saw T. raise his gun and take a snapshot at something in the grass. After he fired, I asked him what he had fired at.

He replied: "Oh, a pretty little thing with two white stripes down its back. It's wounded, I think." Then to the dog: "Go on, old boy —go on!" "Old boy" went on, but suddenly turned away with a howl, and made off, pawing desperately at his nose.

At the same time I noticed T. hastily put his gun down and draw out his pocket-handker-chief, which he applied to his nostrils. On coming up myself, I was saluted by the most diabolical stench I ever experienced before or since.

On the farm-hand being appealed to, he told

us it was a skunk, which had taken the only means of defence (*offence*) it possessed. It was certainly a powerful weapon. I never thought that the organs of scent could be assailed with such force. I remember once a tin of putrid tripe exploding in the midshipmen's berth of the old *S*——, a paddle-flapper I had the honour of serving on board; *that* was bad enough, but the skunk eclipsed even it.

After our adventure we returned to the house. The farm-hand had spread the news, and we came in for a lot of chaff, with many injunctions to keep well to leeward. On our drive back to Niagara we visited General Brock's monument and the battle-ground where the action between the British and American forces was fought in the last war with the United States—I think, in 1812, the British being the victors. The day was a red-letter one with most of us, and was often referred to during the remainder of the commission, always with the dispute as to who was the biggest peach-eater.

Years afterwards my topmate, T., was First-Lieutenant of a corvette on the Australian station. The first time she visited Melbourne I lost no time in bringing him to my Melbourne home, where we sat for hours fighting our battles over again with my wife as an amused listener.

CHAPTER X

WE left Niagara two days afterwards on our
return journey. The Prince was expected the
next day, but we could not wait, as we had to
rejoin our ship. The Canadian Government
had hired a handsome furnished residence for
His Royal Highness and suite, and he stopped
several days, visiting all the points of interest.
On the homeward voyage I heard the Prince
declare that the visit to Niagara was the most
interesting of all his experiences.

We reached Toronto the day after our leaving
Niagara, and embarked on board a fine river
steamer for Montreal; passed Kingston and
the Lake of a Thousand Isles, where we were
enchanted with the scenery. We shot La Chine

Rapids above Montreal, which was most exciting. A group of us were right forward as the great steamer, under a full head of steam, took her course down the torrent. Two men were at the wheel under the vigilant pilot. We looked down at a rock in midstream, on which the steamer seemed to be rushing to destruction, but a spoke or two of the wheel, and she whirled past it. I think the fellow who first took a steamer down the rapids was an exceedingly plucky one. After our experience, our respect for fresh-water sailors was considerably increased.

We stopped two days at Montreal, where we were shown all sorts of kindness, and took our passage on board the *Passport*, the steamer which had attracted our notice during our trip up the St. Lawrence with the Prince. After a jovial night on board with some travelling Americans, we reached Quebec about eleven o'clock, and rejoined the old ship after a trip that I look back on as the most enjoyable in my life.

We found the *Nile*, with its Admiral, had sailed for Halifax, Sir Alexander Milne having had the misfortune to lose one of his sons, who died at Admiralty House, Halifax, during his father's absence.

A few days after our return we left for Halifax with our consorts, the *Ariadne* and *Flying Fish*. Hosts of people came off to bid us God-speed, as the men and officers of the Royal Canadian Squadron had become exceedingly popular with the genial inhabitants of Quebec and neighbourhood, and had made many friends. As we weighed and proceeded down the St. Lawrence under steam, we saluted the province with twenty-one guns, manned rigging, and cheered, and finally Quebec faded in the distance as we made good way down the river.

On entering the Gulf of St. Lawrence we had a stiff blow from the north-east, in which the *Hero's* mainyard was slightly sprung. We were then off Anticosti Island and a lee-shore, and had an anxious time for a few hours until we got steam up—a long process in those days. The wind moderated shortly afterwards, and we made the northern entrance to the Gut of Canso,

THE PARLIAMENT BUILDINGS, QUEBEC, THE OFFICIAL RESIDENCE OF THE PRINCE OF WALES DURING HIS STAY IN QUEBEC

through which we passed, and arrived at Halifax without further mishap

At Halifax we got our mainyard fished; it stood very heavy weather in the Atlantic afterwards, and was a fine piece of workmanship. All our time was taken up in refitting and filling up with stores.

The Prince was to embark for the homeward voyage at Portland, Maine, U.S., on October 20, and the squadron was to arrive there on the 17th. We left Halifax for Portland on October 13. We were this time under the command of the Admiral, who was to see us all safely from his station. We had a good passage down to Portland, and the squadron anchored off the town. We were crowded with sight-seers every day we were there, and entertainments were given to the officers on a most lavish scale. It was the first time most of us had been in the United States, with the exception of our brief journey at Niagara.

One impression, I remember, struck me at the time; it was only a boyish one, certainly. It was the—to me—curious fact of all these crowds of people speaking English, though they were not subjects of the Queen. But if the Americans have a republican form of government, they showed on this occasion the greatest veneration for anything relating to royalty.

The keenest interest was shown by the numerous visitors in viewing the Prince's cabins, especially his sleeping one. There used to be crowds—generally ladies—looking at the royal cot. "My!" they would ask. "Does he really sleep there now?"

The stewards found that the fair Americans evinced something more than curiosity as they snipped off pieces of curtains, sheets, table-cloths, etc., to treasure up as mementoes. In fact, one enterprising lady went so far as to cut a slit in the royal pillow, from which she abstracted a few fists of feathers, doubtless to be distributed as relics amongst her friends and acquaintances.

In the meantime the object of so much reverence was winning golden opinions from all classes in the States. The Prince travelled as Baron Renfrew. He visited President Buchanan at Washington, and the great American hero's tomb. It was a historic and pathetic scene, the great-grandson of the monarch to whom these great territories once owed allegiance, standing at the grave of the man who wrenched them from the British Crown. It touched the Americans greatly. I have no doubt that act of the Prince of Wales was the means of cementing the feelings of brotherhood that kept the Northerners from an open rupture with Great Britain when the sympathies of the latter were given to the Southerners, and I am certain that the graceful act will still be remembered now that the principal actor in it fills the throne of George III.

His Royal Highness visited New York, where he was entertained with magnificent hospitality, which was repeated at Boston. He reached Portland on the morning of October 20; a fine reception was given him, and addresses of welcome presented. At 3 p.m. His Royal Highness stepped on board our state barge, and was pulled off to the *Hero* amid the thunder of salutes from the shore and ships. As he stepped on to the quarter-deck of the *Hero* he was

23

H.R.H. the Prince of Wales again. He looked well and bronzed from outdoor life, and as he bowed and shook hands with the officers we felt very proud to have him in our keeping again.

Immediate preparations were made for sea. The days were closing in at that time of the year, and we looked forward to a rough voyage across the Atlantic.

CHAPTER XI

Homeward bound—Stormy weather—The *Ariadne* tows the *Hero*—Divine service under difficulties—Heavy squalls —"Wait for the *Hero!* wait for the *Hero!* she's a long way behind!"—A digression—The *Hero* once more in tow.

AT 5 p.m. on October 20 the Royal Squadron weighed and proceeded to sea. The *Hero*, with the Prince of Wales's standard flying at her main-topgallant masthead, led the way, followed by the *Nile, Ariadne, Styx,* and *Flying Fish.* It was to the Americans an imposing sight, a British fleet, with the heir-apparent to the throne on board, in their waters. As we passed the fort at the entrance to the bay a royal salute was fired. The *Hero* did not return it, but the *Nile* did, gun for gun. A strange contrast was presented by the two salutes, the American one being slow and in such bad time that it called for the sarcastic remark of our gunnery Lieutenant that "he supposed they had sent up to town for more powder," while the flagship's return was as regular as a clock-beat. However, the compliment was paid in good taste, and if the Americans were not as good at a salute as a British flagship, they had enough powder-burning in the next few years to satisfy the most exacting gunner.

The squadron passed Cape Elizabeth about 5.30 p.m., off which the *Nile*, *Styx*, and *Flying Fish* parted company with many signals of farewell and good wishes, the *Hero* and *Ariadne* being left to pursue their voyage home. The Admiral was proceeding to Bermuda with his ships, and they were soon lost in the gloom.

As we got well in the offing the weather looked wild and threatening in the extreme, the wind being about north by west. Shortly afterwards we made sail, with two reefs in the topsails. Whilst the men were aloft a heavy squall struck us, with rain and sleet. As I came down the main-rigging from my duty in the maintop I got it right in the back, and thought it a very nice outlook for our homeward voyage.

"Flying Fish"   "Arıadne"   "Nile"   "Hero"   Cape Elizabeth Lighthouse

We were now fairly at sea, our royal freight on board, with his suite, all well, and thoroughly satisfied with the trip. It was the duty of the *Hero's* officers to convey His Royal Highness back home, and to pay no attention to personal discomfort or bad weather until that was done.

The Prince had an additional passenger with him. This was Lord Hinchinbrook, a young Guardsman who had been travelling in the States at the time of His Royal Highness's visit. I believe he had been very ill. The Prince, with his usual kindness of heart, had invited him to join his party, and a cabin was found for him on board the *Hero*.

Sunday, the 21st, was passed quietly, the Prince and suite attending Divine service. The follow ing morning we had still the wind abeam; as the *Ariadne* was close astern, the Prince and suite amused themselves with writing on a blackboard and holding it up to our consort, who replied. Captain Vansittart brought his beautiful frigate so close that you could read the various questions and answers without a glass; in fact, some of our officers thought it a little too close.

24

The Commodore was below, and once the *Ariadne* approached so near that the men on her forecastle cleared aft to be out of the way of falling spars. Just then the Commodore came on deck, and when he saw the position of the two ships he stood literally aghast.

"Oh!" he said, as soon as he recovered himself. "Oh, oh! where's the officer of the watch? Oh! where's the signalman? Here, bend an 'open order'!"

As he spoke he made a run aft and jumped on the taffrail, and waved both his arms frantically to the *Ariadne*. As the "open order" signal went up, the Commodore breathed a little more freely; but there was no danger with Captain Van, as he was affectionately called. He was as fine a seaman, if not the finest, the British Navy could produce, and the *Ariadne* was under perfect command all the time.

I must confess that I was in a blue funk myself. I was only a young midshipman of fifteen, and had not served with the Captain of the *Ariadne*, as I afterwards did; then I learnt what he could do. I do not think that the

Commodore could be called over-cautious.   He
had a tremendous responsibility on him with the
Prince on board, and could take no risks.   We
still kept the wind abeam all that day, and well
into the night, when it began to fall light.   I
thought that we might escape bad weather.

I renewed my acquaintance with old " Twenty
Stun," who told me that he was " werry 'and-
somely treated by the Americans—werry 'and-
somely."   Also, " 'Ow had I got on ?"   I told
him all our adventures, to which he was an
attentive listener, and ended up by saying " he
was werry pleased to 'ear I enjoyed myself," and
that he was " werry glad that we were going
'ome again."

The wind remained fairly steady until Monday night, when it fell calm, with cold foggy
weather.   We got up steam and proceeded, but
our rate was slow.   Somehow the *Hero* appeared
out of trim; perhaps it was the bump she got
and the loss of her forefoot.   We were under
steam until the 26th, when the Commodore
signalled the *Ariadne* to take us in tow.   We
got as much top hamper down as possible,

pointing yards to the wind. The *Ariadne* steamed up ahead of us, and sent a hauling line on board by veering a breaker or small cask astern, which was cleverly picked up from our forechains, and the hawser, a fifteen-inch hemp one, hauled on board and secured on our main-deck.

The *Ariadne* soon had us dragging along at over nine knots ; to show what a ship she was, the speed was increased to eleven knots that afternoon. It was a fine feat to tow a heavy line-of-battle ship at that speed in mid-Atlantic with a heavy swell on. I doubt if it could be surpassed even now in these days of high horse-power. I hove the log myself, so I can speak with some certainty.

On Saturday morning, the 27th, the hawser parted on board the *Ariadne* with a tremendous snap, flying clean over her taffrail. Luckily, the men were kept away from it, or it might have done damage. We immediately made sail to a light wind from the north-west. In the afternoon it increased to a fine breeze, and we were reeling off ten knots. As the night came on, the wind got more to the west and increased to a gale, to which we took down reef after reef.

Sunday morning found us reduced to close-reefed topsails, reefed courses, and storm stay-sails. The old ship rolled along—and she could roll, too!—doing about ten knots. After divisions, Divine service was held on the main-deck, with the howl of the gale overhead. The Prince and nearly all the suite attended. We got on all right, although the Rev. Charles Pratt, our chaplain, had some difficulty in holding on to his Union-Jack-covered reading-desk. The service had proceeded as far as the Communion Service, where the responses to the Commandments are sung. Our schoolmaster, who acted as choirmaster to our choir of boys, was beating time, and had just got to the words, " and incline our hearts," when there was an incline of another sort. The old *Hero* had got a rolling fit, and had got it very bad. She gave a tre-mendons roll, the tell-tale indicating 40 degrees. There was an awful smash, and the whole of the marines came down like one man.

I may mention that the seats of a man-of-war church were, in my time, capstan-bars laid across fire-buckets. The buckets at one end of the bars had come down, and there was an inclined plane of Joeys affectionately holding on to each other to prevent themselves tumbling over in a heap. There was a titter of laughter from the row of midshipmen, which was checked by a stern glance from the Commander, who always had this mischief-loving crew under his eye at church; but before he could look round again there was another awful roll, which was accompanied by a resonant crack, and old " Twenty Stun," holding on to his chair with one hand and Prayer-Book in the other, sailed down like a catapult from somewhere, charged through the officers, clutched at a stanchion, missed it, and came back again. The chaplain narrowly escaped being capsized, and thought it better to bring the service to a close by hastily pronouncing the blessing, and the men were piped down.

All that afternoon the wind kept increasing, and the ship walloped along. The Prince was on deck enjoying the novel sight, the great Atlantic rollers chasing the ship and curling over from time to time in a smother of white foam. Our consort, the *Ariadne*, was under shorter canvas than we were, showing only a close-reefed maintopsail and reefed foresail with fore staysail. She was rolling heavily, too, and throwing her forefoot clean out of water when she rose on the sea, and sinking almost out of sight in the trough. To me, and I think to most seamen, there is a wild feeling of exultation at a following gale, especially when you are homeward bound. Such expressions as " The girls at home have got hold of the tow-rope " are indications of the feeling. The stronger the breeze the more pronounced it is.

As night fell the *Ariadne* was close astern of us, but the weather became thicker. Monday morning found the conditions much the same, with the addition of heavy squalls. About eight o'clock one of them came down on us with hurricane force; the reefed fore and main courses were split from clue to earing. We were lucky that our fished mainyard stood the strain.

It was my morning watch, and Lord Kil
coursie immediately proceeded to secure the
remains of the sails, and sent me down to
acquaint the Commander. But there was not
much need to tell that alert seaman that something had gone wrong on deck; he was literally
jumping into his clothes.

"What's gone, youngster?" he said.

"Fore and main courses, sir," I replied.

"Go and tell the Commodore," he answered.

The Commodore's cabin was not far off. I
lost no time, and was returning to the quarter-
deck when the Commander rushed past me up
the ladder. As he did so, I noticed two pale
blue strips hanging down from under his
monkey-jacket; they were a pair of fancy-worked
braces, and he had forgotten to button them up.
As soon as he got up on the poop he took
charge.

"Both watches, shorten sail!" was his
order.

I still was looking with wondering eyes at the
fancy braces.

"Now, Mr. Gough," he roared, "what are

you looking at me for? Go up to your top and look after those men on the mainyard."

As I sprang up the Jacob's-ladder to get into the weather main-rigging, the wind almost pinned me down; but before I made a run up, I took another look at the Commander. A roar of, "Move up that rigging, young gentleman!" followed by the remark to the officer of the watch, which I heard quite plainly—"What's the matter with that boy this morning, Kilcoursie? He's been staring at me ever since I came on deck. What's wrong?" His lordship took a look at the Commander. "He's probably been admiring your fancy braces, sir," he replied, with a smile. The Commander looked round; he was a great stickler for dress. "D——n the thing!" he said. "I never noticed them. No wonder he stared."

New courses were bent, and a pretty tough tussle we had with them. As soon as bent they were set again; we wanted to make as much of the fair wind as we could. The Prince came on deck for a blow before breakfast, and it was a little lesson in seamanship for him, for we were in the middle of it when His Royal Highness appeared. He seemed to enter into the spirit of it all and enjoy it.

The *Hero* continued to drive along before the gale all Monday, and we were congratulating ourselves on what a fine passage we were making. The *Ariadne* kept her station with some difficulty. She was always ranging up on one quarter or another, and although she was only showing her close-reefed maintopsail, with reefed foresail and fore staysail, she could not keep astern of us. As Monday night fell, the gale abated somewhat, and we took a reef out of the topsails. Tuesday morning, the 30th, dawned, but the *Ariadne* was nowhere to be seen. I remember being sent up to the maintopgallant masthead with my telescope to have a look for her. The glass I had was a particularly good one, by Dollond, and was a present from an aunt of mine. I had a careful look round first, but not a sail was in sight. I was told to remain up, and keep a good lookout for our consort. It was as much as I could do to hang on aloft and use the glass at the same time. I would survey the great vessel rolling about underneath me, and then have another glance round. As I had a firm belief in the *Hero's* sailing powers, I was inclined to think that the *Ariadne* was astern of us, although most of the officers maintained that she was ahead, and had run past us in the night. About ten o'clock the Prince and some of the suite came on deck. I noticed His Royal Highness taking a good look at me in my elevated perch, and several of the suite also honoured me with a survey through binoculars. Shortly afterwards another mid came up to relieve me, and we had a yarn together on the crosstrees.

" Well, Gough," said my messmate, " where's the *Ariadne ?*"

" Astern," I replied.

" What will you bet ?" returned he.

" A day's grog," I said.

" All right, old man," he laughed; " you're bound to lose."

" We'll see," said I, as I went down the topmast rigging.

On arriving on deck I found the Prince on

the poop, to which I made my way to report to the officer of my watch. The Commander was also there. As I turned away from Lord Kilcoursie, His Royal Highness addressed me. "I suppose you found it very windy aloft, Mr. Gough," he remarked, with a smile.

"Yes, sir," I said.

"I wonder you managed to hold on. Did you not find it difficult?" he continued.

"No, sir," I replied; "I am always aloft."

"Yes, I know," said His Royal Highness, "but not always in such weather as this."

At this stage the Commander took up the running.

"There is not much danger to that young gentleman, Your Royal Highness; he can hang on like a cat," was the remark.

As I made my way down the poop-ladder I thought what sort of a cat *he* would make at the main-topgallant crosstrees in a heavy gale. About seven bells (half-past eleven) I was sent up again, and began to look round, especially astern. As I did so, my eye was caught by a glimpse of a sail in that quarter, but I lost it again the next minute. I reported it on deck, and a sharp-eyed signalman was sent up to me. As he was coming up the rigging I caught the sail again in the field of my glass, and kept it there. The sun shone on the canvas, and I could see it easily. The signalman also saw it, and it was a frigate's foretopgallant sail. I came down and reported. As I passed my messmate I informed him that I had won my bet, as I was certain it was the *Ariadne* that was astern of us, and coming up. This turned out to be the case, and there was much signalling done. It appears she thought she was running past us in the night; but the contrary was the case, and we left her behind.

I may here mention that there was at that time a popular song called, "Wait for the Waggon." A clever parody of it was made up by some wag on the *Ariadne's* lower-deck, with the chorus altered to

> "Wait for the *Hero*, wait for the *Hero*,
> She's a long way behind."

When we came home it was sung in Plymouth,

and a good many free fights between the two ships' companies took place on shore as the result.

In addition, the *Times* correspondent on board the *Ariadne* gave it a prominence in his account of the Prince's tour and voyage. The officers were chaffed about it a good deal, and the same song once gave a brilliant young woman an opportunity of airing her wit at my expense. Perhaps I may be permitted to relate the story.

After our arrival home, the officers all got a few weeks' leave. We mids each made a bee-line for our respective paternal halls. I have no doubt all our dads and maters thought us very great fellows. I know mine did; for boys of fifteen or so to have been so intimately brought into contact with royalty was a great honour. Royalties were not as plentiful in those days as they are now, and much less was seen of them. Many of the Royal Family were then in the nursery. When I got home, I found my dad was going to celebrate my arrival in the good old fashion by a big dinner to the whole countryside. I was the eldest son of the

family, and he was going to show me off to
the county, and many were the welcomes and
invitations I received from all sides. In fact, if
I had not been a midshipman I might have
begun to fancy myself a person of some importance and put some " side " on, but any such
thing as " side," as it is now called, was promptly
cured in the *Hero's* gun-room by a few feet of
the port-tackle fall—an infallible remedy, never
known to fail after the second application.

However, the fatted calf was killed, the 1820
port trotted out, with some wonderful East
Indian Madeira that had been twice round the
Cape, and only brought out on very special
occasions. On the day the great spread was to
take place I had been out shooting. When I
got home our old butler informed me that
Miss ——, the young lady who was afterwards
to air her wit, had arrived to stay for a few
days. She was a great friend of my mother's,
and was generally an acquisition in any country
house—very handsome, rode to hounds, could
handle a rifle well, played, sang, and danced to
perfection; in fact, she was a slap-bang-all-

round girl; no home was ever dull when she was to the fore. One of her accomplishments was a happy knack of improvising on any theme. Her name—well, never mind, but her family once gave a not very popular Governor to Victoria. As the guests assembled in the drawing-room preparatory to dinner being commenced, my dear old mother came up to me.

"Tom," she said, "I want you to take Miss —— in to dinner. She wants to hear all about your trip" (the young lady being the one I have mentioned).

"All right, mother," I replied, nothing loath.

I was beginning to think that I would be told off to some old dowager. My lively companion and myself brought up the tail end of the procession to dinner. Soon after we were seated she opened up the conversation by saying:

"Well, Master Tom, I suppose you had a great trip to Canada with the Prince of Wales?"

"Yes," I replied, "we had a very good time."

"So I have heard," she continued; "we read all about it in the papers; but what a slow ship the *Hero* must be!"

"Slow!" I said; "why, she's the finest ship in the service."

"Oh yes," was the reply, "all you midship men say their ship is the finest. The other day," she went on, "I was stopping at the C. H's." (some neighbours of ours), "and their son had just been paid off, I think they call it, in the *F——* from China. He said that she was the finest ship in the service."

"The *F——!*" I said, with great disdain; "why, she's only an old paddle-flapper!"

"What's that?"

"A paddle-wheel steamer," I explained.

"Oh, indeed!" was the answer, followed by the question, "What about that song?"

"What song?"

"'Wait for the *Hero*.' Very funny, was it not? I read all about it in the *Times*."

I mentally anathematized the busybody of the *Times*.

"Do you remember the words?" she went on.

"I have forgotten them," said I, inventing a white lie for the occasion.

26

"Indeed," my companion said; "perhaps I could supply some others."

"I have no doubt you could," I replied; "but I don't see the necessity.'

Just then the ladies retired, and the gentlemen joined them shortly afterwards. I noticed my dinner companion busily engaged in a corner of the room, but she came forward as we came in. Presently she was asked by my mother to sing, and I was hunted up to take her to the piano. I lit the candles, opened the instrument, brought forward the music, and asked her what she was going to favour us with.

"A little composition of my own," she said, as she sat down, struck a few chords, and broke into the then well-known air, "Wait for the Waggon," to which she put an amusing parody on the *Hero's* trip, with the chorus—

> "Wait for the *Hero*, wait for the *Hero*,
>   She's a long way behind "

—at the end of each verse.

It was certainly very clever, but very confusing to me, who stood by the piano looking like a fool amid the laughter of my father's guests. I believe "Wait for the *Hero*" was sung round the countryside long after she was paid off. I may mention that the midshipman who had been paid off in the paddle-flapper joined the *Hero* shortly after I returned from leave, when we used to chaff each other about the young lady.

I am afraid I have left the *Hero* in mid-Atlantic whilst I have transported my readers to my home. On November 1 it became quite calm, but with a heavy swell. Once more the *Ariadne* was signalled to take us in tow. This time we got an eighteen-inch hawser aboard and made good progress. In the meantime the gun-room mess was working up an event of some importance. This was a dinner to His Royal Highness, and great were the deliberations amongst the seniors about the entertainment. It was arranged that the dinner should be on one of the last days of the voyage, and at our present rate of progress we ought to arrive at Plymouth about the 10th. It was decided to invite His Royal Highness for his birthday,

the 9th.   The invitation was graciously ac-
cepted by the Prince and Major-General Bruce,
his Governor.   Our sea-stock was getting low,
but our caterer interviewed Mr. Parkes, the
Prince's messman, and obtained an assortment
of American tinned delicacies to supplement our
stock.   It was proposed to have a large piece of
salt junk, flanked by a piece of salt pork and pease-
pudding, on the table, just to give His Royal
Highness a glimpse of Admiralty goose and
turkey, as it was termed.   I forget whether it
was put on or not, but I think it was vetoed at
the last moment.

We continued in tow of the *Ariadne* until the
morning of November 4, when a breeze from
the south sprang up, to which we made sail.
On the following day the wind shifted to east-
south-east, right in our teeth, and increased to
a gale.   Our prospects of reaching Plymouth
by the 10th were now hopeless.   We had nothing
to do but beat dead to windward, making to the
north-east on the starboard tack.   The weather
became bitterly cold, the wind coming more to
the east as we thrashed away at the head seas

under treble-reefed topsail and courses. Under such short canvas we made little or no way on our course, but there was no help for it; steam in such a head-wind was out of the question and we had a short supply in our bunkers.

CHAPTER XII

His Royal Highness proves a good sailor—Lord St. Germans gets a nasty fall—Preparations for the gun-room dinner—The last dinner in the cabin—Presentation of medals—The Prince's birthday dinner in the gun-room—The *Hero* ships a sea—His Royal Highness and General Bruce get a ducking.

IT was November 6, a bad time of the year to be working to windward against an Atlantic gale, but we had to make the best of it. The wind blew with a persistence that was provoking; if it shifted at all, it was only a point or two more to the eastward, and we had to keep farther away from our course; in fact, instead of heading for the English Channel, the old ship's nose pointed as if she were making for the North of Scotland. The Commodore was constantly on deck looking at the dog-vane, and seemed to worry a good deal. I heard afterwards that the cause of his annoyance was the anxiety that the

prolonged passage would give the Queen and
Prince Consort. It could not be helped. It
looked as if old Neptune was loath to give up
the Sea-Queen's heir now that he had got him.
The impression was still further heightened by
the wind dropping from a gale to a stiff double-
reefed topsail breeze, still dead against us, a
gentle reminder to keep at sea.

In the meantime the illustrious object of so
much attention from the sea-god took it with
the utmost good-nature. The Duke of Newcastle seemed to treat the head-wind as a
personal grievance, and looked very sour on it.
He would make his appearance on the poop
every afternoon, and pace up and down with his
private secretary in solemn silence. As he
went down the quarter-deck ladder after his
constitutional, he would give a haughty glance
up at the sails, round at the quarter-deck and
guns, ending up with the midshipman of the
watch, doing his tramp under the lee of the
main trysail, as much as to say, "What the
d——l do you mean by it all?"

Old Lord St. Germans, who took it with a

good grace, would wrap himself up in an immense blue cloak with a great cape, and come on deck. He evidently felt the cold keen wind very severely. The same blue cloak was nearly the means of creating a vacancy in the peerage. It was at evening quarters, or evening muster, as it is now termed, and the Prince and most of the suite were on deck.

I previously stated I was midshipman of the quarter-deck quarters. We were waiting for the retreat to be beaten, and I was standing close to the weather poop ladder, when a dark object hustled down it, and landed on the quarter-deck with a heavy sump. It was poor old Lord St. Germans. He had attempted to come down the ladder, the wind blew the cape over his head, he missed the hand-rail, and came down as I have described.

How on earth the old gentleman escaped being killed I can't imagine. It was a serious thing for a man of his age (quite seventy) to have such a fall. I at once ran to his assistance, and got the cape from over his head. I got him on his feet. His Royal Highness, with his usual solicitude for the welfare of others, was one of the first down the ladder, and anxiously inquired if his lordship was hurt. But the old gentleman was as staunch as a game-cock; with my assistance he struggled to his feet. " Thank—Your Royal Highness—I'm —not—at—all—hurt," he gasped out as he caught his breath; but I could see he was badly shaken. I assisted him to the hatchway, then down to the main-deck, where the sentry got his valet to take him to his cabin. He was such a charming old gentleman, and had endeared himself to all of us so much by his gentle and courteous manners, that we would have regretted deeply if anything had happened to him.

In the meantime preparations were going on apace for our gun-room dinner to the Prince, and anxious calculations were made by us youngsters as to whose afternoon watch it was going to be on that eventful day. We were only boys, and, remembering who our guest was, we were wild with excitement. I was beginning to wonder what they were going to give His

Royal Highness to eat. Sundry pieces of salt-junk had appeared on the gun-room table—a bad omen as regards sea-stock—but our caterer was a wise old party, and kept his own counsel. We were always hungry, and the ship's provisions were good enough, in his estimation, to satisfy our cravings.

The invitations we received from time to time to dine with the Prince were regarded from different points of view—the honour and a jolly good dinner. I would not like to say which was put first by a midshipman on a course of salt horse. I have a strong recollection that the result was a dead-heat.

I well remember the last dinner I had in the cabin. I sat next my friend, Major Teesdale. An old campaigner like him knew what a hungry boy could put away. With a merry twinkle in his eye, he recommended every dish that was handed round. At dessert there were some glass dishes of delicious French dried fruits. The Major quietly pulled them close to the edge of the table, and during the conversation would slip a handful of the fruit under the cloth, then into my hand, and from there it went into my tail-coat pocket. As we rose from the table, and I made my bow to His Royal Highness, I was in such a state about the ballast I carried in my pockets that I made a sidelong bow, and cannoned against a chair, capsizing it, at which His Royal Highness roared with laughter, the Commodore regarding me with astonishment. Perhaps he thought I had too much champagne on board; but it was not the fluids, it was the solids, that were my trouble. On reaching my chest in the steerage I disgorged my treasure. It was my middle watch that night, and my masthead friend and myself shared the preserved fruits under the lee of one of the quarter-deck guns.

The 9th of November arrived at last, in spite of head-winds. It was the Prince's nineteenth birthday, and we hoisted his standard at the main-topgallant masthead with white and blue ensigns at the fore and mizzen. At twelve o'clock a royal salute was fired from the main-deck guns, and repeated by the *Ariadne*. A double allowance of grog was served out to the ship's company to drink health, long life, and many happy returns of the day to our royal passenger. In the forenoon His Royal Highness distributed medals commemorating his visit to Canada. The little act was done in quite home-like manner. All the mids went up one by one to the Commander's cabin, where the Prince was attended by Major Teesdale. As my turn came, I arrived breathless from a rush up the lower-deck ladder. His Royal Highness laughed at my excitement.

"Well, Mr. Gough," he said, "do you want a medal?"

"Yes, sir, if you please," I answered.

"Teesdale, where's Mr. Gough's medal?" asked His Royal Highness.

Major Teesdale began looking on the table, where the medals were laid out. I believe he was slow on purpose, to have a joke with me. The Prince went over to the table.

"Why, here it is, just in front of you," he said, taking up the case.

"So it is, sir," replied the Major.

His Royal Highness handed me the medal, for which I thanked him.

He added as I left the cabin : " Mind, I want all your photographs."

" Oh yes, sir," I returned, as I jammed my cap on my head, preparatory to making a run down to the gun-room to examine my treasure. The medal was enclosed in a blue morocco case with the Prince's feathers embossed outside; inside was a small strip of paper with " Mr. Gough, from A. E.," written on it by His Royal Highness. The medal itself was a beautiful piece of work, by Wyon, and it is now amongst my most precious relics. A representation of it appears on the cover of this book.

But the event of the day was our gun-room dinner to His Royal Highness. It was also decided to tack at four o'clock, and make a long stretch to the south. It would have been better for our entertainment if the tacking business had been postponed for a couple of hours or so. The dinner was to take place at three o'clock, the mess being cleared at one o'clock to allow the stewards to lay the table and make every-

thing ship-shape. A council of war was held
by the seniors as to the safety, or not, of leaving
the stern-port open with the sash in. The
lower-deck ports were barred in, and there was
a fine smell of marine about the gun-room which
would not have exactly the same effect as a
bitter to those unaccustomed to it.

One of our mates, however, agreed to sweeten
the air before the Prince came down. This he
did by a couple of windsails down the after-
hatchway. It was decided to have the stern-
port triced up, and leave the broadside ports
shut. The gun-room being on the starboard
side, it was the weather one, the ship being on
that tack. At 2.45 the mess was thrown open,
and we all assembled. Of course we were in
full rig, tail-coats and white waistcoats, the
mates wearing their undress coats and scales.
We had the band on the main-deck to play
" The Roast Beef." The gun-room looked as
well as the stewards could make it; the two
8-inch guns and carriages lashed along the
waterways, fore and aft, were converted for the
time being into a buffet, on which dessert was

laid out, and the open stern-port gave a good light, which was supplemented by a swing-lamp at the fore end of the gun-room.

At three o'clock the band struck up "The Roast Beef of Old England" (precious little of it about just then). The Prince and General Bruce were received on the main-deck by the two senior mates and escorted down to the gun-room door, the passage from the lower-deck ladder to there being kept by our marine servants, each holding up a battle-lantern. The door was thrown open, His Royal Highness received by the full strength of the mess, and conducted to the seat of honour on the right of the president, whilst General Bruce occupied the seat to his left. The dinner was a first-class one; it was a perfect revelation to us all, the good things our caterer got. Of course everything was preserved —soups, meats, vegetables, etc.—but full justice was done to them. The Prince took everything that was going; laughed, chatted, and joked away, free from any restraint. He was amongst boys and young men of about his own age. The dear old General fell in with the spirit of the moment, his face beaming with good-humour. Then the cloth was cleared away.

After the formal health of the Queen was honoured, our senior mate proposed the health of our royal guest, conveying to His Royal Highness in a quaint, humorous speech, full of good points, all the best wishes of those present. The toast was drunk standing, with great cheering and waving of glasses. His Royal Highness returned thanks in a few charming sentences, and General Bruce returned thanks also in a few flattering words. After we resumed our seats the conversation proceeded, the Prince listening to some of our seniors' experiences with great interest. Stories of service in the Crimea, China, India, and other parts of the globe were brought forward for His Royal Highness's amusement.

Everything was going as merry as a marriage-bell when we heard a commotion on the lower-deck. Our head-steward told Mr. Vice in a low tone that it was only both watches turned up to " tack ship." It had been arranged that the midshipmen of the afternoon watch would look after the duties, so that our dinner would not be disturbed. We did not bother our heads about what was going on on deck.

Presently the ship became upright as she hove in stays. Tacking a heavy line-of-battle ship under short canvas in half a gale of wind is not like tacking a fore-and-aft schooner. The ship does not "fore-reach" in stays, and is as likely as not to get stern-way on before she fills on the opposite tack. As I said, everything was going as right as right could be, when there was a downward plunge of the *Hero's* stern. All that was seen outside the sash of the stern-port was a green opaque mass. The next instant a volume of water burst in like a waterspout, pouring over the table, washing away dessert, decanters, glasses, and everything movable in one common jumble. The president of the mess had his chair knocked from under him, but managed to hold on to the strong table. The Prince and General Bruce were drenched to the skin, and there was about three feet of water swirling about all over the deck. The stern-port was hastily lowered with a heavy clap. By

28

the dim light of the swinging lamp His Royal
Highness was assisted to the gun-room door,
laughing heartily at the end-up of the dinner.
Poor General Bruce, as he passed out, the water
dripping from him like a wet swab, managed to
gasp out, "Many thanks for your dinner." I
wonder if His present Majesty ever remembers
the drenching he got on his nineteenth birthday
in the *Hero's* gun-room.

As soon as the Prince was away a party of
marines were set to work to bail out and swab
up the water. The scuppers had been plugged;
remains of dessert and broken dishes were washing about. As the marines cleared up, various
finds of raisins, almonds, preserved fruits, etc.,
were picked up and readily put away by them;
a little salt water rather improved the flavour.
Amongst other fruits that shared in the wash
away were some fine Spanish olives. One of
the marines, groping about, picked up a fistful
of them; he took them over to the lamp
to examine them. When he saw what they
were, he took a bite at one and looked at it
again.

"What have you got there, Bill?" said another Joey.

"Blessed if I know," he said; "some sort of green plum; but"—taking another bite—"I'm jiggered if they don't take salt mighty quick!"

So ended our great dinner to the Prince.

CHAPTER XIII

THE 10th of November found the *Hero* on the port tack, making her southward stretch. It was the intention of the Commodore, if the wind continued adverse, to stand well down into the Bay of Biscay, so as to have our port well under our lee if a fair wind sprang up. I should say we were, at the time we tacked, about four hundred miles or so off the west coast of Ireland. The wind came more to the north, being about east-north-east, and the *Hero* made a south-east course. We did not lay so close up to the wind as the *Ariadne*, the reason being that the *Hero* had hempen shrouds, the *Ariadne* wire ones. The consequence was that the *Hero's* massive rigging prevented her lower yards from being braced up as sharply as the *Ariadne's*, the difference being nearly a point in favour of our consort.

The 11th and 12th of November saw us still on the same course. There was not so much sea on as we got closer in towards the French coast, but the wind continued strong until the evening of the 12th. There were no exciting events on board, except a little sport that took place on the lee side of the *Hero's* quarter-deck.

I have, during my time, had various kinds of sport at sea and on land, but only once has it fell to my lot to have a woodcock hunt on the ocean ; this actually took place on board the *Hero*. It was in the forenoon, and I was midshipman of the watch. The Commodore was on deck, walking up and down with the officer of the watch, when suddenly a bird flew over the weather-hammock nettings, and fluttered down into the lee scuppers. For a moment or two I hardly noticed what sort of bird it was, but a second glance showed it to be a woodcock. I come from a part of the old country where that bird is considered the pick of game, so you may be sure that I lost no time in making a dash at it.

The Commodore was a keen sportsman, and saw what the game was at once.

"Cock, cock! by G—d!" he shouted, bounding down the poop-ladder. "Quartermaster, bring a broom, and we'll have him!"

The quartermaster of the watch, a sedate old seaman, stared from his perch at the conn. The unwonted commotion attracted the notice of the afterguards, who were sweeping up decks, and a general hunt took place. The poor bird was quite exhausted, and could only hop and flutter about. The stately Commodore, myself, and the men bumped up against each other in our endeavours to secure the game, which was ultimately triumphantly hauled out from under one of the guns by an afterguardsman and handed over to the Commodore, who was as pleased with his prize as a child with a new toy, and carried it off to show the Prince. I suppose the bird was blown off the land by the easterly gale. It was very poor, and could not have gone much farther. I do not remember the ultimate fate of the woodcock, but I think it was brought to port and released on the slopes of Mount Edgcumbe.

On the morning of the 13th the wind dropped and shifted to the north, which we took advantage of to lay farther up towards our port. During the day the wind still continued to veer more westerly, and on the evening of that day died away altogether, but sprang up from the south-west during the night, a fair wind at last, with drizzling rain and mist. The morning of the 14th saw the *Hero*, with a fine wind on the port quarter, reeling off ten knots under a cloud of canvas. We were then to the south-west of Ushant, close into the land by dead reckoning. We had not had an observation for the two previous days, but we kept the old ship at it for all she was worth. A fair wind after a spell of head winds, and your homeward port under your lee! What a glorious thing it was to be a sailor in those days!

Everyone was jubilant, from the Prince down to the second-class boy. At 8 o'clock that night we hove-to to get a cast of the deep-sea lead. It was my last dog-watch, and I had the glory of getting the men placed from the cat-head, fore-chains, sheet-anchor, main-chains, mizzen-chains, right aft to the weather-quarter. As the big lead was let go, the call of "Watch there, watch!" rang out from the various stations, the coils of the line dropping from the hands of the men. The reel stopped running, and the soundings were called by the quarter-master, "Ninety fathoms!" The lead was brought forward to our Master, Timothy O'Sul-livan, to have a look at the arming—"Soft sand and shells." The English Channel is so accurately surveyed that a ship's position may be fairly well told by the soundings and nature of the bottom. As I entered the gun-room and announced the glorious news a cheer broke from the mess, followed by a shout from the senior mate to the steward as to how much rum he had.

In those days every member of the mess drew his allowance regardless of age; if you were thought too young, the mate of your watch did you the honour of putting your half-gill away for you. In the present instance there was enough rum to make a big bowl of punch, which was duly brewed and served out. What a row there was in the old *Hero's* gun-room that night! toasts, songs, etc., were given with uproarious applause. A favourite song in midshipmen's berths of that day was "Spanish Ladies"—a fine old sea-song with a rousing chorus; the words are to be found in Captain Marryat's novel, "Poor Jack." On this particular occasion the words of the chorus, "From Ushant to Scilly is thirty-five leagues," were highly applicable, and they were roared out without calling for any request from the ward-room to "the gun-room officers to make less noise"; in fact, an extension of half an hour before putting the lights out was asked for and granted by the Commander.

As we expected to make the Lizard Lights in the morning watch, a sharp lookout was kept by everyone on deck. About four bells in the middle watch a number of rockets were seen to the north-west of us, which were answered by a gun and blue lights in an opposite quarter. We fired a rocket and burnt a blue light, but kept on our course.

We learnt, on our arrival in Plymouth, that the rockets and blue lights were shown by a search squadron sent out to look for us, consisting of the *Orlando*, of the Devonshire first-class steam reserve, the *Gorgon*, *Spiteful*, and the celebrated troop-ship *Himalaya*. They had no idea that the answering signals were shown by the object of their search, and they arrived some days afterwards rather crestfallen.

About one bell (half-past four) in the morning watch a shout from the fore-yard, where we had two lookout men, of "Two lights on the starboard bow, sir!" announced that our land-fall was made with good accuracy. The lights were the Lizard Point, and the *Hero* was kept away a point or two. When morning broke, the well-known Cornish coast appeared with its red cliffs, a sight regarded by everyone with feelings of delight. As each well-known landmark came in sight, as well as a few red-sailed trawlers, pretty well all hands came up to have a look.

The Prince was on deck highly pleased, the Duke of Newcastle's sour looks had vanished, and he unbent enough to compliment the Commodore on the excellent land-fall we had made. Old Lord St. Germans, beaming all over his face, appeared in his big blue cloak; he was like a schoolboy getting home for the holidays. Even old "Twenty Stun" was up to have a look at the shores of Old England. He informed me that "he was werry pleased to see the land again," and that "he once thought we would never get 'ome." He asked me what time we would be in. When I told him about ten o'clock, he said "he 'oped to be in town to-night, and would be werry pleased to be in a steady bed again—werry pleased."

As the *Hero* proceeded steam was being got up. Off Rame Head we turned the hands up, shortened and furled sails, lowered the screw, and went ahead under steam. We hoisted our number at the fore, the Prince's silken standard flying from the main. As we steamed along the coast we were evidently signalled. About ten o'clock we passed the western end of the breakwater, and a few minutes afterwards anchored in Plymouth Sound, twenty-six days out from Portland, and a little over four months from the time we had left England.

Immediate intelligence was sent to the Queen and Prince Consort of the safe arrival of the Prince of Wales from his interesting tour. The news was received throughout the kingdom with a sense of relief; our protracted voyage had caused a feeling of anxiety in the minds of the public.

On board the *Hero* immediate preparations were made to disembark the Prince and suite. The first to pay their respects were the Port Admiral, Sir Houston Stewart, and the General commanding the Western District, the Admiral's yacht being sent out for the Prince. About eleven o'clock a farewell gathering of the officers was held, His Royal Highness shaking hands with everyone, the suite also saying good-bye. At 11.15 yards were manned, guard and band up; the Prince descended the *Hero's* gangway into our state barge, and was pulled over to the Admiral's yacht, his standard slowly fluttering down from our main royal masthead.   Curious to say, as if loath to come down, it caught on one of the backstays, and was torn in half.   I remember securing a piece of the silk from the rigging to keep as a relic.

As the yacht started for the shore a royal salute was fired by the *Hero* and *Ariadne*.   The yacht steamed round the old ship, the men cheered, and the officers on the poop stood bareheaded; the band struck up "Auld Lang Syne," followed by " Rule, Britannia," His Royal Highness waving a last farewell to those he had honoured as a shipmate.   As the steamer receded in the distance a final wave of the Prince's handkerchief was the last glimpse we got of him.   Our duty was finished, but we were sincerely sorry to lose him.

CONCLUSION

The visit far-reaching in its consequences—The first pulse-
beat of the Empire—Honours in connection with the
visit—The *Hero* in commission—Her ultimate fate—
An old sea-dog's memories—*Vivat Rex!*

THE safe return of the Prince of Wales from
his Canadian tour was hailed with satisfaction
throughout the kingdom. From every point of
view it had been a conspicuous success, and
called forth the most favourable encomiums
from both sides of the Atlantic. The Canadians
had been delighted with the gracious act of Her
Majesty in sending the Prince to visit them.
President Buchanan addressed a letter to the
Queen, in which he paid the highest compli-
ments to the Prince's tact, amiability, and
demeanour during his intercourse with the
people of the United States.

There is no doubt in my mind that the visit
of the Prince of Wales to Canada in 1860 was

of far-reaching character, little thought of at the time, but now showing its fruits. I believe that it called forth the first beat of that pulse of Nationality and Empire which is now throbbing with such mighty vibrations round the globe. It gave His present Majesty the first insight into the vast possibilities of the great Empire over which he now rules.

I am certain that during the past forty years His Majesty has, by his quiet influence, been a potent factor in bringing about the present satis factory relations of the Colonies with the Mother Country. I look upon him, apart from the kingly office which he fills by right of birth, as an astute, far-seeing statesman of the highest order, to which the nation is under a load of gratitude which it will be hard to repay, and I would prove myself a poor prophet if I did not predict that under the rule of King Edward VII. the British Empire will enter into a career of prosperity still greater than that which we now enjoy.

The Colonies will never experience again the contempt and indifference with which they were once regarded by some statesmen. It is difficult at the present day to realize the extent of that feeling, but to illustrate the pitch to which it once attained, I remember that when I was in New Zealand a good many years ago, a Member of the House of Representatives tabled a motion to the effect that, owing to the neglect of Her Majesty's Government, the New Zealand Government would approach the people of the United States to take over the colony. I think we may assure ourselves that such an experience as the above will never occur again.

To return to the Prince's arrival at home, I will mention the rewards that were conferred on some of those who took part in the tour. The Duke of Newcastle was made a Knight of the Garter; the Commodore was appointed to the command of the *Victoria and Albert*, the royal yacht; the Commander made a Post-Captain; the two senior mates, Lieutenants; engineers and assistant-paymasters got a step, and a formal letter of thanks from the Lords of the Admiralty was read to the officers and ship's company, the latter being given three weeks' leave.

Shortly afterwards, the *Hero* steamed into Hamoaze, the ship's company were hulked, and the ship docked at Keyham, where the extra cabins were removed, guns mounted, and the *Hero* restored to her normal aspect as a man-of-war again. A new Captain, Alfred P. Ryder, was appointed to the command, a new Commander, and officers to replace those promoted, joined, and the *Hero* took her place with the Western Division of the Channel Fleet. The old ship took part in the cruise of the squadron round the British Isles in 1861, when we visited Leith, the Orkney and Shetland Islands, and Glasgow; we then escorted the Queen and Prince Consort from Holyhead to Kingstown when they visited Ireland that year. From there we went to the west coast of Ireland, finally returning to Spithead in November. The *Hero* was suddenly ordered out to reinforce the North American and West Indian Station in consequence of Commodore Wilks, of the United States Navy, in the *San Jacinto*, boarding the Royal Mail steamer *Trent* in the Bahama Channel, and taking from her by force the Con

30

federate States Commissioners to the Courts of London and Paris.

The act was a gross breach of international law, amounting almost to an act of war, and was received by a storm of indignation from one end of the kingdom to the other. Lord Lyons, the British Ambassador at Washington, was instructed to demand the return of the Commissioners, together with a suitable apology; in the event of refusal, to demand his passports, and retire to Halifax. Luckily, the good sense of the American people prevailed. They saw the serious predicament their headstrong officer had placed them in, and the Commissioners were given up with a good grace, but it was a very near thing for a short time.

The *Hero* arrived at Bermuda in January, 1862. The first news we received when we arrived was the death of the Prince Consort, which took place a few days after we left England. The *Hero* visited Halifax again, where we met many of our old friends, and finally, was ordered home to pay off in October, 1862.

*   *   *   *   *

Our second homeward voyage across the Atlantic was very different to the one with the Prince on board when Neptune tested his courage. No sooner had we got clear of Halifax Harbour than a fair wind sprang up, which continued all the voyage, and we made the passage from Halifax to Spithead in eleven days—a wonderful performance at that time, one which showed that the *Hero* had lost none of her sailing qualities, in spite of the *Ariadne's* song of "Wait for the *Hero*."

We were ordered round to Sheerness to dismantle and pay off, which we did on November 22, 1862, after being three years and eight months in commission, of which I served the whole. She was a happy, jolly ship from the day she hoisted the pendant until she hauled it down.

I only saw the old craft once again. Some years afterwards I was again at Sheerness, and was sent up the Medway to Chatham in a steam-launch on some duty. Coming downstream I was attracted by the appearance of one of the hulks lying up in ordinary, out of the fairway. There is not much to distinguish the various

ships lying up; they are all painted the usual
dockyard, duckity-mud colour, now in the height
of fashion as " khaki." As I looked at this
hulk, her lines seemed familiar to me. " The
old *Hero*, by Jove!" I said to myself. " Go
along that line-of-battle ship," said I to the coxswain of the launch. As the bowman hooked
on, I looked up at the side I had so often been
up. A single tarry old rope hung down like a
long snake. I got hold and swung myself up.
As I did so the warrant-officer in charge, a
frowsy old carpenter, attracted by the noise of
the fussy little steamer, put his head over the
gangway to see what all the rumpus was about.
As I landed on the old ship's quarter-deck he
touched his cap to me.

" What might you please to want, sir ?" he
asked.

" Not much," I said; " but I served a commission on board this ship, and I would like to
take a look round again."

" Certainly, sir," he replied. " Will I go
below with you ?"

" No, thank you," I returned. " I think I

know my way about, and I can trice a port or two up."

"Very good, sir," said the old fellow, with a touch of his cap.

As I stood on the old planks again I looked up. Alas! where were the towering masts, with their well-squared yards and the taut rigging up which I had so many times sprung? I pictured to myself the clouds of swelling canvas, the Prince's silken standard flaunting upwards with its gorgeous quarterings, or the long pendant soaring aloft as it whipped the wind. I went to the after-hatchway and down on the main-deck. I remembered the crash of the band, the Prince and his suite, the bull dances we used to have. From the main-deck to the lower-deck, by the light of the scuttles, I made my way to the gun-room door and threw it open. As I triced up the very port that let in the sea that drenched the Prince, a flood of memories came to me of the happy years I had spent in the mess, but the place was no longer peopled by the crowd of jolly laughing boys, and the only sound was the lap of the yellow tide round the rudder. I let the port down again and got on deck. I thanked the old carpenter, and went down the side.

The launch shoved off, and began to puff away. As I stood up in the stern-sheets to have a final look at the old craft, the coxswain touched his cap.

" Beg pardon, sir," he said, " but that's the *Hero*, isn't it ?"

" Yes," I said, " that's the *Hero*—the ship that took His Majesty to Canada and brought him safely home."

" I had a messmate last ship who served the commission on board her," said the coxswain. " She was the happiest ship in the service, he told me, sir."

" Yes, she was," I replied, " the happiest ship in the service."

It was the last I saw of her. In the course of a few years she gave way to the new order of things, and was sold out of the service to be broken up.

My land readers may wonder at the regard the sailor bears for his old ship, but the craft that has been his floating home, that has borne him over the surging seas, and whose decks he has paced in fair weather and foul, has always a claim for his love and veneration.

The events I have been relating took place nearly fifty years ago, and of those who took part in them, how many are left? The principal actor in them, is now His Majesty King Edward VII. Long may he reign! Of his suite, few, if any, are alive. The Duke of Newcastle died suddenly a few years afterwards. Lord St. Germans, Major Teesdale, Dr. Acland, and others, their places know them no more. Of the ship's company of the *Hero*, 880 officers and men, the Commodore, Commander, all the Lieutenants with one exception, and nearly all the others are sleeping their last watch below— some in quiet country churchyards, others in the deep, others in strange countries, waiting the last pipe from the Great Skipper, when all being true sailormen will be sure of good billets in the new quarters.

When I look back on the many better men who have gone before me, I wonder at the mystery of life, and why I am here. From the time I was seventeen until I was over thirty my life was a constant series of hair-breadth escapes from death. I could relate adventures that would excite De Rougemont's envy, and that would fill a good-sized volume. Most of my experiences were in Spanish South America and the South Pacific. I have been through the Pacific Islands to New Zealand, from Panama to Cape Horn. I have seen cities here to-day, gone to-morrow, a mass of ruins only, showing the devastating effect of a great earth-quake. I was always in the thick of it, and wonder, when I look back on those times, how and why I came through clear; but the life had strange fascinations.

Sometimes on a Sunday in summer, when I am sunning myself on my veranda (for I am as fond of the sun as a lizard), I lie back in my big chair looking at the blue mountains in the distance, and smoke myself into dreams. Old times come back to me, and I fancy I hear the rush of the gale, the dash of the wave, and feel the plunge of the ship. Or the wind in the

LIEUTENANT THOMAS BUNBURY GOUGH, R.N.

To face page 236

honeysuckle over my head turns to the whisper of the soft trade-wind amongst the feathery cocoa-palms on the shores of some Pacific island, beautiful as an isle of the blest, and I hear the boom of the surf on the outer reef. Then an almost uncontrollable longing comes over me to see these scenes again, but I pull furiously at my old pipe when I realize that such is not for me : my day is done. I have but my memories left, the proudest and the happiest of them that memorable cruise with the gallant boy Prince, now His Gracious Majesty Edward VII.

Vivat Rex!

INDEX

Lightning Source UK Ltd.
Milton Keynes UK
UKHW02f0857250918
329457UK00007B/945/P